Conclusive Evidence

A Novel
By Al Macy
AlMacyAuthor.com

Chapter One

CRIMINAL DEFENSE LAWYERS SEE bad people at their best, while family lawyers see good people at their worst. It's a cute saying and a good conversation starter at cocktail parties, but my family law clients aren't so easily classified.

On December 3, 2018, Horace Scully arrived at Goodlove and Shek with an attitude. My daughter, interning with me while on a break from law school, showed him into my office. With all her fingers extended, she touched the middle one to her chin then turned her hand toward me: American Sign Language for "good luck." Nicole had learned ASL to communicate with her aunt but got a kick out of using it for sending me secret messages. She was twenty-four, tall, with long dark hair, a button nose, and a deservedly confident look. Chuckling, she went back to the reception area.

I came around my desk and put out my hand. "Garrett Goodlove. Nice to meet you, Mr. Scully."

To give him the benefit of the doubt, I don't think he saw my offer of a handshake. He stormed over to the window, where he stood taking deep breaths. *Trying to calm himself?*

"Relaxing view, isn't it?" I sat down behind my desk.

I'd purchased the office suite back when I was an arrogant, overpriced criminal defense lawyer. On the second floor of a Victorian building constructed in 1889, the window overlooked Redwood Point Harbor. The start of commercial crab season had been delayed once again, so most of the crab boats sat in their slips looking like depressed dogs whose afternoon walk has been canceled.

The office had the solidity of a London men's club, with dark wood paneling, a fireplace, and a Persian rug courtesy of a merchant I'd successfully defended against a charge of manslaughter.

When Mr. Scully had calmed down enough to speak, he stepped over to my desk and dropped a sheaf of papers on it. He stabbed it with his index finger so hard I worried he might break it. "I spent my hard-earned money to have a lawyer write up this contract, and now I'm told it isn't worth squat. Unenforceable."

Scully was around thirty, with the kind of not-quite-a-beard whiskers that down in San Francisco might have been considered stylish. Here in Humboldt County, the look usually meant that the face's owner hadn't gotten around to shaving. Scully's brown hair was neat enough but suggested he cut it himself, perhaps using one of those handheld haircutting devices—a Robocut? His permanent scowl would take a gallon of Botox to repair, and the absence of laugh lines

2

suggested that Horace Scully was rarely a happy camper. He wore a maroon suit jacket over a black shirt. Good quality stuff, but I caught a whiff of eau de thrift store when he dropped into my visitor chair.

"How can I help you today, Mr. Scully?"

He leaned forward and jabbed his index finger down on the contract again. "Out of the goodness of my heart I was a sperm donor, and apparently now I'm on the hook for child support! I shouldn't be—we all agreed. Read this contract."

I picked it up and flipped through it. "This will take a bit of time. Would you like some coffee?"

"Is it free?"

I frowned. "What?"

"It's not something you're going to tack on to the fees, is it? Like when the hospital charges you twenty dollars for a Tylenol."

I frowned again, trying to read his expression. Was he joking, or was he from another planet?

"You're in luck," I replied. "Totally free. Today only. If you want cream, however …"

The humor was lost on him. "No. Black, thanks."

I pushed the button on my intercom. "Sweetheart, could we have two coffees, please?"

One of Scully's eyebrows jumped at the word "sweetheart."

"She's my daughter," I said.

"Smart. Good tax benefits."

"Are you an accountant, Mr. Scully?"

He nodded.

I took a few minutes to read through the contract. The meat of it started with:

"WHEREAS, the parties intend for Molly to be inseminated with Horace's sperm in the hope that Molly will conceive and give birth to a child or children;

"WHEREAS, the purpose of this Agreement is to set forth the parties' understanding of their respective rights and obligations with regard to any such child or children born from the insemination so that no misunderstandings arise in the future ..."

I finished reading it. "This is a well-written contract." I recognized the style of an attorney and friend who had recently retired. Family lawyers in Redwood Point, a town of only 30,000, were a close-knit group, and we often worked together to solve our clients' problems.

"But it won't hold up in court, will it?" Scully asked.

I put the contract on my desk and leaned back. "Why don't you start from the beginning?"

He took a deep breath. "My twin brother was Keith Scully."

"Was?"

"I'll get to that. Five years ago, him and his wife, Molly, wanted to have a child. They couldn't. He had low sperm count or something. We were all good friends back then. Not any longer."

I could relate to that. My twin sister and I had been estranged for years. Ever since—*no, don't think about that.* I clenched my teeth.

"Hello? Mr. Goodlove?"

"Sorry. Please continue."

"So, we were all good friends back then. Keith and Molly came to me. It would be perfect, they said. Since Keith and I were identical twins, the child would be the same as if Keith was the father. Much better than if they got some anonymous donor, understand?"

"Clever," I said.

He continued with the story. He had made it crystal clear that he wanted no obligations, financial or otherwise. He loved his twin but wanted any monetary support to be optional. A reasonable request.

The insemination worked, and Molly gave birth to a healthy baby girl. Everyone doted on her, including Horace. The monkey wrench came from an inheritance dispute resulting from Keith's will. It was written by a lawyer who knew nothing about wills. The hapless trio fought bitterly, and Molly and Keith stopped talking to Horace. The emotional storm might have blown over but for a tragic car accident. The baby, properly snugged into her car seat in the back, was unscathed, but Molly received major injuries. Keith was killed.

"I'm very sorry for your loss, Mr. Scully."

He pressed his lips together and nodded. "Now Molly is in debt and is coming to me for money."

"May I ask about your financial situation?"

"I've been a good saver all my life," he said. "I'm incredibly frugal and careful with my money. I've always lived below my means. Way below. For example, I only get the very basic cable. I hate monthly expenses; they really add up. I was married briefly, but my wife was like Molly—couldn't stop spending money. Luckily, I divorced her before it was too late, and I dug myself out of the financial hole she'd put us into."

"Would you care to tell me your net worth?"

He puffed out his chest. "Almost two million dollars."

"What's your feeling toward Molly now? And your niece?"

"The girl is very cute, but it doesn't matter. It's the principle of the thing. We all decided that I wouldn't be providing child support, but now that she needs more money, she's coming to me."

"Wouldn't it feel good to help them out?"

He crossed his arms. "I will help, but I don't like to be forced to. It's not fair."

I chewed on my lip. Horace Scully didn't need a lawyer, he needed a shrink. His frugality had overwhelmed his common sense and his heart like a loyal servant gone bad. It wasn't my place to tell him that, however.

I sighed. "Here's the thing, Mr. Scully. The courts are reluctant to let adults contract away the rights that belong to a child. Children are not property, and the courts will always put the children's best interests first. Could I gently suggest that you think along those lines? What's the child's name?"

"Hortense."

I almost laughed. A terrible name, but I saw the significance. "Ah, they named her after you. You might want to reconsider pursuing this. Take some time, spend time with Molly. I'm sure—"

"She needs the money now."

"It will be expensive to take this to court." I pointed to the contract. Maybe I could appeal to his tight fist rather than to his sense of compassion.

"It's the principle of the thing."

"Right." My first instinct was to tell him to get another lawyer, but perhaps I could come up with something that would work out for everyone.

I paged through the contract. "Well, there's a chance you could prevail. You did everything right. I see you used SemTech for the insemination. When was the girl born?"

"Uh ..."

"What?"

"SemTech, uh, didn't ..."

"You went with a different company?"

Horace stared at me.

I froze. "You didn't just—"

"Do you know how much they charge for this kind of thing?"

"But Keith and Molly were going to pay."

"I convinced them to go the natural way."

"You and Molly just ..." I was tempted to ask whether Horace's twin watched. Or was part of the action. "Keith was on board with that?"

"Of course! What do you take me for?"

I pushed the contract over toward him. "Your case just fell apart. As far as the courts are concerned, you had an affair with Molly. Your sister-in-law is going through a real tough time. I'm sure your brother wouldn't have wanted her to be suffering like this. You could help her."

"It's the—"

"Right. It's the principle of the thing." Much of my income came from people fighting for the principle of the thing. "Do you love your niece? Do you spend time with her?"

"That's beside the point."

I closed my eyes, trying not to think about my niece. About …

"Mr. Goodlove?"

I shook my head. "Sorry. There are a few things I can pursue. I'll send you a contract, but I hope you'll change your mind and not follow through. Are you sure you're the father?"

He scoffed. "Of course I am. Keith was infertile, and we could never prove it anyway, like with DNA or something, because we're identical twins."

I stood and walked Mr. Scully out to reception. "I'm going to look into a few things, and if you still want to go ahead, we'll discuss our options."

We shook hands and he left.

Nicole looked up from her MacBook. "Big case, Dad?"

"Not terribly. Why did you wish me luck?"

"Oh, the guy was just kind of freaked out. Like he'd worked himself up. Melodramatic."

I smiled. "Not like you."

"What do you mean?"

"You have your melodramatic moments."

"Name one."

I leaned against the wall. "Uh … I seem to remember when you wanted to go to San Francisco with that guy Rudy, and your mother and I—"

"Ha! I'm an adult now, Dad, in case you haven't noticed. That was when I was a teenager. It was my *job* to be melodramatic." She put on a Valley Girl accent. "Like, hello! I'm, like, a grownup now. Totally. Did you, like, *forget* or something?"

I laughed and put my hands up. "Okay, okay. You know I'll always see you as my little girl. But I'll stop. I'm working on it."

"If anyone around here has to work on his emotions, it's—oh, Dad, I'm sorry. I shouldn't have said that." She stood and walked over to me. Gave me a hug.

"No, it's perfectly okay."

"You're recovered now. I know that."

The door burst open. Nicole and I both jumped.

My twin sister, Carly, stood there, shaking. We hadn't communicated in years.

In ASL she said, "Angelo is dead, and the police say I murdered him."

Carly and I are fraternal twins, meaning that the marketing department in our mom's ovaries decided to put on a two-for-one sale, squeezing out a pair of eggs at once. As a result, not one but two of Dad's happy-ass sperm cells achieved their lifelong goal of fertilizing an egg. Carly and I look no more or less alike than any other two siblings, we just happened to pop into this world on the same day.

Carly often hears the phrase: "You're too beautiful to be deaf." It might sound like a compliment, but it drives her up the wall. I, on the other hand, give hearing people the benefit of the doubt. I can forgive them, guys especially but women too, for saying something phenomenally stupid when they first encounter her star-quality looks. It's a shock, especially here behind the redwood curtain. The beautiful people tend to emigrate from Humboldt to their natural habitat—Los Angeles, Paris, the Mediterranean. I give the average

Joes around here credit for being able to put a few coherent words together when they run into my sister. Carly, however, doesn't suffer fools gladly.

I've been waiting for someone to tell me I'm too handsome to be a lawyer, but it hasn't happened yet. "You're too old to be Carly's twin" would be more likely. I have enough laugh and frown lines for both of us. My eyes aren't as blue as hers, but they work pretty well for staring down a witness. I'd lost a fair amount of hair, but in a good way, with a healthy peninsula of gray-brown hair that's holding its own, making me look like a drill sergeant.

My face has a priceless quality to which I attribute part of my success as an attorney: I look smart. You can't tell a book by its cover—take Einstein for instance —but "you look like a smart guy" is something I've heard often enough. It can be a curse, too. Sometimes you want your opponent to think you're a few files short of a full briefcase. With that in mind, I've actually practiced in the mirror, trying to look like Goofy from the Disney cartoons: "Garrett Goodlove for the defense, Your Honor, ga hilk."

Carly and I were born a few minutes apart in 1975, making us both forty-three. Through the luck of the genetic lottery, she'd been afflicted with a gene mutation causing nonsyndromic hearing loss. "Nonsyndromic" means that there aren't any other signs or symptoms of the genetic mutation. The only thing her lottery ticket won her was profound deafness. I was spared. I'm not even a carrier.

I'd be in big trouble if I referred to it as an affliction or even a disability in front of Carly. She doesn't see it as such. I understand her point of view, but growing up beside her deafness made me appreciate my sense of hearing more. Don't tell her I said that.

Our parents were smart. After some hand-wringing following the discovery of Carly's deafness, they researched the subject exhaustively and met with experts. Above all else, they wanted to choose the right path for Carly's education.

In 1880, a conference of educators declared that sign language should not be taught to the deaf. Instead, students should learn to lip-read and speak. Alexander Graham Bell used his wealth and fame to push this point of view, known as "oralism." Although it seemed to make sense—how could it be wrong to teach kids to communicate with those in the hearing world?—the declaration was a disaster for generations. Students forbidden to sign were denied a rich language, and their education, and their self-esteem, suffered. In the late 1900s manualism made a well-deserved comeback.

Armed with their newfound knowledge, our parents picked up our family and dropped it down in Redwood Point, California, 270 miles north of San Francisco. The small town was home to the country's top school for the deaf, Bizet University. Bizet used a combined approach to deaf education.

Our parents had taken a crash course in ASL and began teaching it to Carly and me when we were six months old. They told me Carly picked it up faster than I did, something that doesn't surprise me. Later on, I taught it to my wife, and the two of us had passed it on to our kids.

There she stood, in her trademark button-down office shirt with the top two buttons undone. Her gray pencil skirt showed off her figure, and black heels accentuated her dominating height. She'd taken off her leather jacket and draped it over a chair. Carly, a freelance journalist, was the strong twin, so it worried me to see her upset on that drizzly afternoon in December. After a hug, the first time we'd even touched in years, we stepped into my office.

I wanted to find out what had happened, sure that it wasn't as serious as Carly thought, but first, I needed to put on my lawyer hat.

"Before you tell me what happened," I signed, "there are a few things—no, wait, Carly, let me finish—there are a few things you need to know. Everything you say here is confidential. Neither Nicole nor I can reveal anything you tell us without your permission. Even if I don't end up representing you, we can't—"

Carly slapped my desk then signed, "Of course I want *you*."

"Wait!" I said, frowning. The sign for "wait" is both hands in front of you a few inches apart, palms up, fingers wiggling.

Our conversation was totally silent. "I am *not* the best lawyer for this case. I've been out of the criminal defense business for a while. Jen is smarter than I am, and there are probably some hotshot attorneys from San Francisco who could do an even better job." Jen was the Shek in Goodlove and Shek.

Carly looked like an angry pit bull. "No. You."

I turned to my daughter. "Nicole, you observe only, okay?"

"Should we bring Jen in?" she said.

Jen had the rare combination of a heavy-duty intellect and a work ethic that put the stereotypical Asian overachiever to shame. If this turned out to be a murder defense, her knowledge of case law would be invaluable.

After thinking about it, I made the sign for "no." "Let's wait on that. I don't want to have to translate everything we say." Turning back to my sister, I started again. "Finally, Carly, let me describe a hypothetical situation. A client comes in and tells me that he ... shot his neighbor—"

"I didn't kill Angelo." Carly was breathing hard.

"Let me finish! If a client admits to a crime, there are certain things I can't do. I can't put him on the stand and have him lie, for example. That would be what's called subornation of perjury." I fingerspelled the final phrase.

"Don't lecture me," Carly said.

"This is what I tell all of my clients, okay? Not just you. Now tell me what happened."

She started her story. "Detective Crawford and some other cop showed up at my door an hour ago."

"*The* Detective Crawford?"

"Of course! How many are there?" Carly's lack of tolerance for fools extended to her twin brother.

Damon Crawford interpreted the phrase "protect and serve" as "convict and screw over." He had an us-versus-them attitude when it came to the public—the police versus civilians. I doubted he was assigned this case by luck. He probably weaseled his way into it as soon as he heard that Carly was involved. Their paths had crossed before, to his detriment. This was his chance for revenge.

Carly tapped me on the shoulder, bringing me back to the present.

She said, "Some surfers saw Angelo fall from Tepona Point into the ocean."

"Tepona Point? Remind me."

"You know. Just north of Camel Rock."

Got it. It was a ridge that jutted out into the Pacific. A short trail along a knife-edge takes you to an ancient split rail fence that keeps the tourists from danger. Climb over that and you can get a selfie on the cliff edge cantilevered over the ocean. Depending on the tide, a fall would either put you into the sea or into the morgue.

"I'm sorry, Carly." I leaned forward and took her hand. She and Angelo were separated, with little chance of reconciliation—well, none now—but I was sure it was a blow for her to learn of his violent death.

"Wait," she said. "They didn't find his body."

"Then how did they know he was the man who fell off the cliff? The surfers were far away. I'm surprised someone even noticed, actually."

"His car was in the parking lot."

I put it together in my head. "So, a surfer paddles in, calls the police, says he saw someone fall off the cliff. They go to Tepona Point, see his car, and assume— what?—that you pushed him off? How did they come to that conclusion?"

"I'm a person of interest."

I let out a breath, relaxing for the first time since Carly came charging into the office. "Of course you're a person of interest. You're his wife. That doesn't mean they think you murdered anyone. You're jumping to conclusions."

"I'm not. I can tell. Crawford has already decided that I killed Angelo." Carly was an amazing judge of body language. Perhaps many deaf people are. But she was taking her hunch too far.

"But you said they haven't even recovered the body."

"The swells are running eighteen feet. I saw the Coast Guard helicopter hovering out there. No body yet."

"Okay. So we don't even know for sure that Angelo is dead. Maybe he just went for a walk. Someone or something else fell off the cliff." I didn't believe that, but saying it might let Carly relax a bit.

Or not.

"What?" she said. "He parked at Tepona Point then went for a walk along the road? You can't get to the beach easily from there. Give me a break, bro. I hope you're just saying that. I don't think you're that stupid."

I glanced at Nicole. She was taking it all in and doing a good job of keeping her hands in her lap.

I looked back to Carly. "What did you say to the police?"

"Nothing."

"Good. Keep it that way. How did you communicate?"

"The usual way. I had him speak into my tablet, and I typed in my answers. The tablet converts my typing into speech. You've seen that, right?"

I hadn't. Carly could speak pretty well. Easily well enough to be understood. But she didn't. She knew from the reactions she got that it sounded funny, as if she were retarded or something. That was unacceptable to her. Also, she told me that once she spoke, people somehow jumped to the conclusion that she could hear fine. They would stop looking at her when they talked to her, for example.

"Does the app you use keep a record of the conversations?"

"Yes."

"Show me," I said.

She bristled, probably because she valued her privacy, then pulled out her tablet and put it on her lap.

"They came to the door and asked to come in. I said no. They said they were very sorry, blah, blah, then something like, 'We have reason to believe your husband, Angelo, may be dead.'"

Carly is an excellent speech-reader, or lip-reader as hearing people say. However, most hearing people don't realize that speech-readers can rarely understand more than thirty to fifty percent of what is said. Carly's on the high end of that, filling in lost details from the context. They would have watched her reaction closely, of course. Carly was a stoic person, and a subdued reaction could be taken the wrong way.

"How did you react?" I asked.

Carly mimed a posture of extreme shock, two hands up, fingers splayed, mouth and eyes opened wide.

"Don't clown around! Damn it, Carly, this could be serious. From now on, there'll be no jokes. People can interpret expressions incorrectly." I glanced at Nicole. If she thought her aunt was funny, she was doing a good job of hiding it. I turned back to Carly. "Tell me how you reacted."

"I reacted like someone who was just told that her husband, whom she didn't live with, was maybe dead."

She picked up the tablet, queued up the conversation, and handed it to me.

> Carly: Speak normally, and my tablet will translate your speech into text.
>
> Other: We understand this is hard for you, but we only have a few questions at this time.
>
> Carly: I'm not a suspect, am I? Angelo and I are separated.
>
> Other: You are a person of interest.
>
> Carly: Why?
>
> Other: You are Angelo's wife.
>
> Carly: We're separated.
>
> Other: Can you tell me where you were this morning?
>
> Carly: You know my brother is an attorney. That sounds like something I shouldn't answer without him present.
>
> Other: You aren't under arrest. We just have some questions.

Carly: I will not answer any questions without my attorney present. Thank you for contacting me.

I nodded. "Good. I wish all my clients had as much sense. Where were you this morning?"

"I went running on Clam Beach, then I walked home."

"Alone?"

"Yes."

"So, right past Tepona Point," I said.

"Yes."

"Did you speak with anyone?"

She gave me a give-me-a-break look.

"It could have happened." Because of Bizet, there's a sizable deaf population in our area. She could easily have seen a deaf friend.

She signed, "No."

"Okay. I want you to sit down and reconstruct your day in detail, on paper. Do it here, and leave the paper here. This will probably turn out to be nothing. Angelo will show up, perhaps. Are you doing okay?"

"Angelo and I were through. We stopped loving each other after … after …" Her shoulders sagged.

I signed, "Maybe there's some good that can come from this. I've missed you, and I hope we can return to the friendship we used to have."

Carly nodded.

"I'll have Louella use her contacts in the police department to find out what's going on."

* * *

The day after Angelo's disappearance, Louella Davis sat at her dining table having a chocolate-covered donut and some afternoon coffee. She tapped the ashes from her cigarette and picked up the *Times Standard*. Her eyes wandered across the page and stopped on the headline: *"Man Falls from Cliff, Presumed Dead."* When she got to the part that stated Angelo Romero may have been the victim, she stopped chewing. *Uh-oh.*

If you lined up a hundred people and asked who looked the least like a private investigator, Louella would win hands down. A black woman of sixty-five years, she looked more like someone's grandmother than a hard-boiled detective. Occasionally, strangers would do a double take when they saw her on the street. It happened once when she was walking beside a friend.

"Did you see that?" she asked him.

"The funny look?"

"Right. Double take. I get that now and then."

The friend laughed. "You know why, right?"

"You gonna tell me?"

He said, "You haven't seen *The Matrix*?"

"No, I saw it. About twenty years ago."

"You look like a character in that movie. The Oracle."

Louella had run her hand through the frizzy hair that fluffed out on both sides of her head. "The older woman? Huh. I don't really see it, but okay."

She had brown eyes and dark freckles across her cheeks. Her reading glasses usually sat low on her nose or hung from a beaded chain around her neck. The grandmotherly facade hid the veteran police detective underneath. She'd spent twenty years in LA's robbery-homicide division then retired to work in the Redwood Point PD. Her nickname, Badger, followed her from Southern to Northern California. She was relentless at digging for information, and she was a lot tougher than she looked. She'd gone private just before the scandal that resulted from an RPPD officer shooting an unarmed man. Lucky for her.

The article said that Angelo's wife, Carly, was a person of interest.

Louella rinsed her coffee cup, made a few calls, and walked the five blocks to Garrett's office. She had a combined home and office near Old Town, between Garrett's office and the courthouse. It was convenient back when Garrett was a criminal defense lawyer and supplied her with most of her work.

Taking a final drag on her cigarette, she climbed the stairs to his office. The man himself was out, apparently, but Jen was in her office with the door open. The two offices had a dog bone floor layout, with the reception area in between.

"You work too hard," Louella said.

Jen startled and looked up. "Louella!" She waved her in.

The two women hugged, and Louella dropped into a visitor chair.

Jen Shek's mother was Japanese and her father, Chinese. Her delicate features always made Louella picture her as a model or actress, not a small-town lawyer. She'd come to the US as a child and was fluent in English, Japanese, Chinese, and, especially, legalese. In her late twenties—it was hard to tell her age, actually —she had a small mouth, small nose, and intense eyes.

Eyes that could drill right through a hostile witness. She'd tucked her shoulder-length hair behind her ears, displaying a pair of jade earrings. Her hair matched the dark brown of her zip-up turtleneck sweater.

"Still smoking," she said.

"Yeah." Louella waved the air in front of her face. "I'm working on it. Down to a couple a day."

"A couple of—"

"How's the boss doing?"

Jen leaned back in her chair. "Better. I've been worried, but it will be okay. He's coming around."

"No more criminal defense cases though?"

"No. I doubt he'll ever go back—I don't know what he'll do with Carly's case." She leaned forward, looking toward Garrett's office even though she knew he was out. "He's lost his edge—maybe that's a good thing. For him, not for the firm."

"Meaning?"

"He's nicer now. When he came back to work, he'd changed. The cutthroat, ruthless, take-no-prisoners attorney we all knew? That guy's gone. He's a lot more lovable now, but I don't think he realizes it. I'm sure being Mr. Nice Guy is better for him, but the edge is missing."

"He started introspecting too much. That's the problem. After Raquel and then Patricia—"

"What do you mean?" Jen frowned.

"I have a saying." Louella took a cigarette from her purse, put it in her mouth, but didn't light it. "The examined life is not worth living. Plato got it backwards."

"It was Socrates."

"One of those guys. Anyway, he said the unexamined life is not worth living. But it's when you start examining your life that you get into trouble. Am I happy? Should I have done this or that? What should I do with my life? Am I a good person? Why did that have to happen?"

"Someone's in a philosophical mood today."

"Yeah, I'll have to watch that. You know who got it right?"

Jen smiled. "Who's that?"

"George Carlin. He asked why people read self-help books. 'Life is *not* that complicated,' he said. 'You get up, you go to work, you have dinner, you take a good crap, and the next day you do it all over again.'"

Jen laughed. "Louella's outlook on life."

"It's my guiding principle, to tell you the truth. I'm just saying that maybe that's what broke Garrett. He was going along fine, living his busy but uncomplicated existence. Then the tragedies hit, and he started examining his life."

"I don't think it was that simple," Jen said.

"Maybe not. So, Garrett's only doing family law now?"

"It fits his new persona better."

"But you're still criminal."

"Someone has to be the prick around here."

They both laughed.

As if on cue, Garrett came through the reception area and into Jen's office carrying some beers and a bottle opener.

Chapter Two

I DISTRIBUTED THE BEERS and sat. "Why are my ears burning?"

My partner's office was like mine but with an exposed hardwood floor instead of a Persian rug. My son's nature photos adorned the walls: shots of the redwood forest or waves crashing against our rugged coast's sea stacks. Her leaded windows weren't quite as tight as mine, allowing some saltwater tang in along with the shrieks of the seagulls.

Louella said, "Jen was telling me you're going soft in your old age."

"Nah." I took a swig of beer. "I just see the world a little differently now. You been out of town, Lou?"

"Because I didn't come sooner?"

"Yeah. You would have heard about Angelo and come right over if you'd been in town."

She put a finger on her chin as if thinking hard. "I coulda been sick or something."

"Not likely. I've never seen you sick."

"Donuts and cigarettes. You should try it."

"Organic?"

"That's the secret." She pointed at me. "The cigarettes are gluten free, and the donuts are non-GMO."

"Any scuttlebutt from your contacts?" Jen asked. Neither Jen nor I needed to say anything about confidentiality. Louella knew she'd be on the case.

"I just flew in today, as Sherlock here figured out. I read the headlines and made a call or two. You know about the eyewitness?"

"Eyewitness?" Jen and I said together.

"I'll take that as a no." Louella rubbed her shoulder. "I heard they have a witness that puts Carly on the trail out to Tepona Point."

I choked on my beer and stood up. "Damn! She told me she was on Clam Beach then walked home."

Louella said, "She lives on Scenic, right? Tepona Point is between Clam Beach and her house."

Jen motioned me to sit down. "You know how eyewitnesses are, partner. Whoever it is could have seen her on the road, but then, when he read the news, thought he'd seen her on the trail. There are lots of possibilities."

I paced. "It's just like Carly to keep something like that to herself."

"Come on, Garrett," Jen said. "You're getting way ahead of yourself."

I sat back down. "You're right. It's too personal for me. Did you hear anything else, Lou?"

"That's it. You know it's Crawford's case, right?"

"Don't remind me."

Louella finished her beer. "What do you want me to do?"

"Try to find Angelo. Pretend that we know he's alive. Treat it like a missing persons case."

"Not likely, given that someone dropped off the cliff and his car was left behind."

"Yeah, but you know me."

"Thorough to a fault." Louella made some notes.

"I'm guessing the Coast Guard is still searching for the body?" I asked.

Louella looked at her watch. "Yeah. It's only been twenty-four hours. They would have shut it down overnight then started again at dawn. They use a program called SAROPS to guide the search. It makes predictions based on currents, tides, and so on."

"How could the body not be found?" Jen asked.

I rubbed the back of my neck. "It's not really that surprising. The swell was over eighteen feet. I'm sure you've both seen it when it's like that. White water all the way to the horizon. And the body would sink, right, Louella?"

"A live person floats because of the air in the lungs. Blow out all your air, and you sink to the bottom. We had a guy near Malibu who floated in a pool facedown. The air never got a chance to pass out of his lungs, and he stayed floating for days. But in that washing machine under Tepona Point, water would have filled his lungs right away."

"But he would have floated after a while," I said.

"Right. Angelo may have been dead, but the bacteria in his gut and elsewhere in his body went right on living. As they consume the body, they produce gases that would bring it back up to the surface. However, the

25

water here is cold, so that could take days or weeks. Bottom line: not surprising that the body wasn't found."

"We may never recover it."

"True," she said.

Jen picked at the label of her beer, the Lost Coast Brewery's Great White ale. "What was Angelo like?"

"That's right, you never met him. What about you, Louella?"

"No, but he had a reputation. Like a borderline criminal."

"Yeah, that's right. He was a slimy guy," I said. "Everyone in the family took turns trying to convince Carly not to marry him. It's a mystery what she saw in him. Maybe it was her contrariness that did it. Push Carly on anything, and she'll push back. Hard."

"And he wasn't deaf?" Jen said.

I nodded. "Yeah, that's the bigger mystery. The deaf culture here is a big part of Carly's life. She's kind of militantly deaf, if you know what I mean."

"No, partner, I don't."

"Sorry. She gets a little fed up with hearing people. Let me give you an example, something I've seen a few times when I'm with her. Someone will say, 'Oh, you're deaf?' She'll nod, and then they'll say something like, 'Oh, you don't *look* deaf. Can you read lips?' She'd nod again, and then the hearing person would talk with exaggerated mouth movements that actually made it harder for her to understand. Those kinds of things drove her up the wall."

Jen frowned. "But they were just trying to help."

"That isn't how she sees it. Carly has always had a bit of a chip on her shoulder. She was teased cruelly as a child, so it's understandable, but she's not a forgive and forget type. She socialized almost exclusively with her friends in the deaf community. I was included because I knew ASL, and I was her brother, but I often saw an us-against-the-world attitude in her social groups."

"Yet she married Angelo."

"Right. She and I were inseparable until Angelo came into the picture. It was love at first sight, I guess, and her deafness made no difference. All I can figure is that it was his bad boy persona that kept her interested. He had some kind of animal magnetism. They eloped when she was eighteen and he was nineteen. Our family freaked."

"But the marriage worked," Jen said.

"Another mystery, but I have to say they did seem to love one another. They were together until … you know."

"What was his job?" Louella asked.

"He went from one moneymaking scheme to another."

"For example?"

"Let's see … I don't know the details, but at one point he was buying high-value luxury cars—Mercedes, BMW, Land Rover—and then shipping them to buyers in China. An exporter would front him the money. Technically, it was legal."

"I'll see what he's been up to lately," Louella said. "What else?"

"You know your job better than I do. I guess you better look into Carly as well. Find out more about that witness. And we'll want to talk to the surfer who saw Angelo fall. There's no budget on this."

* * *

Two days later, we hadn't heard anything more from the police. Still keeping my fingers crossed that Angelo would turn up or that his disappearance would be explained in a way that didn't implicate my sister, I continued on with other business.

A receptionist in the lobby of Agena Bioscience told me that the geneticist would be with me shortly. Located in Santa Rosa, the firm provided both genetic counseling and fertility assessments. No sooner had I sat down than Dr. Olga Magroski came striding across the floor with her arm extended. Around fifty, she had flyaway blonde hair, dangly earrings, and a big smile filled with somewhat discolored teeth.

"I received the material you sent me. It's a very interesting family issue you have," she said after I'd introduced myself. She had a slight accent that I couldn't place.

"Have you ever heard of something like this before?"

"An identical twin as a sperm donor? No. Very interesting."

Molly Scully had provided the results of the fertility tests her husband had ordered, and I'd forwarded them to Agena Bioscience.

I followed her out of the lobby. We passed an impressive lab with the requisite centrifuges, busy bees in lab coats, and those machines with rows of pipettes that you see on the news whenever they do a story on something biomedical. Her office had a nice view of the hills and a desk crowded with folders and journals.

She settled in behind her desk. "How may I help you today, Mr. Goodlove?"

I sat in the visitor chair. "It's pretty simple, I guess. I'd like to know whether Keith could be the father of the child and if there's a way to know for sure."

"The answers are simple, as well. I have the fertility test results here, and they show that Keith had a very low sperm count. It's called oligospermia." She rummaged around in a desk drawer and pulled out a piece of paper. "To give you a feel for it, here's a chart that shows the pregnancy rate plotted against sperm count. Of course, if there are no sperm, then the rate is zero. It rises quickly from there but then levels off. Do you understand?"

"Where is Keith on this chart?"

She took a pen and pointed to a spot on the curve. "He was here, corresponding to a pregnancy rate of less than one percent. If he'd been a little higher, they would have been candidates for intrauterine insemination. They could have done in vitro fertilization, but apparently they chose not to."

"Test tube baby."

She laughed. "Yes. That's right."

"So Keith couldn't have gotten his wife pregnant?"

"Well, it only takes one sperm, so it's always possible, but we're in hit-by-lightning territory here." She laughed again.

"Okay, so unlikely but not impossible."

"Precisely."

"And the second question. Could we tell who the father is?"

"Yes, but not with the standard DNA test."

"But don't Keith and Horace have the same exact DNA?"

"No. With identical twins, the fertilized egg divides a few times and then splits in two. At that point, yes, the DNA is identical. But cells divide millions of times before birth, and during those divisions there will be a certain number of errors made. They're called mutations. So the infants' DNA is no longer identical. And those mutations are passed on to their children. Got it?"

"In general, yes. So why can't the DNA tests detect those differences?"

"Because there are too few. A standard DNA test only looks in a few places in the DNA. But you can run a special test that looks at many locations on the DNA. It's something we could do here."

"And it's much more expensive."

"You bet."

"Does this stuff continue to amaze you?" I asked.

She shut one eye and tilted her head. "What stuff?"

"Oh, mainly that all of the information needed to create a complete human being is coded in this one DNA molecule that's, what, a thousandth of an inch long?"

Dr. Magroski held her arms straight out to her sides, as if being crucified.

It was my turn to cock my head. "What?"

"This is how long the DNA in a single cell is. Two meters long, two nanometers wide, and all jumbled up together in the cell's nucleus. Take all the DNA in all your cells, and stretch it out, and it would extend across the solar system. Twice."

Learn something new every day.

* * *

I wanted to get reacquainted with my twin sister, so I suggested we go surfing, just like the old days. Also, it would give us an opportunity to scope out the view of Tepona Point from the Camel Rock surf spot.

There's more than one sea stack along the coast called Camel Rock. Apparently, ships of the desert are often on the minds of cartographers. The Camel Rock at Houda Point Beach creates an ideal surfing location in the winter months. The waves are big, but a rip current usually forms along the rock, so surfers can take an escalator ride out to the break. When conditions are perfect, there's a consistent right break. The great conditions never result in the types of crowds seen in Southern California, which was another plus. The North Coast is significantly less populated than the more tinselly half of the state, and the water is a lot colder. Unfortunately, the area is a destination resort for a basket of deplorables who travel thousands of miles to be there: great white sharks. Humboldt County has had sixteen shark attacks since 1960, many in the shadow of Camel Rock. Little River empties out there, and that, along with the rocky shoreline, attracts fat, tasty seals. My mantra is that the drive to the spot is more dangerous than the surfing itself, but that rings hollow when I'm sitting on the board, feet dangling above the shadowy abyss. I prefer to make the hour's drive north to Crescent City, where attacks are less frequent, but Carly thinks that is a particularly wussy thing to do. The ASL sign for "chicken" is formed by making a beak shape with your fingers and pecking it down onto the other hand.

I pulled into the parking lot high above the break. It was so foggy I couldn't see the waves. The St. George buoy reported a swell height of nine feet, which is at the upper range of my comfort zone. Carly pulled up while I was still putting on my wet suit. It didn't take her long to catch up. While I wear a full suit with a hood, gloves, and booties, she goes with a suit only. I've never figured out whether the water didn't feel as cold to her or she just toughed it out better. I also wore earplugs to keep the cold water from exacerbating my surfer's ear, a bony growth in the ear canal caused by exposure to cold water and wind.

"How are you doing?" I said. We wouldn't be able to talk on the hike down to the beach, since we needed our hands to hold the boards.

"Anything new?" she asked.

I avoided the question; I wanted to discuss it when we were out on the water. "I'm not worried."

That was mostly true. Without a body, it would be harder for the prosecution to argue that Angelo was dead. But not impossible. Most people think you can't convict someone of murder without a corpse. Not true, unfortunately.

I put my longboard—yellowed from age—on my head and followed Carly down the long set of railroad-tie stairs. We got to the beach and walked into the water. When the size of the waves became apparent, I hesitated. Carly smiled and made the sign for "chicken." Then she made the sign for a particular part of the female anatomy.

I sighed and followed her out into the waves. We got on the conveyer belt, but the sailing wasn't as smooth as

I liked. I had to turn turtle for some of the breakers. Carly's board was smaller, letting her duck dive under the approaching foam. We got out to the lineup and joined two other surfers. The first thing I did was to look north to Tepona Point. Not visible. Too foggy. But it hadn't been foggy on the morning of the third of December.

A nice wave came around the point, and Carly went for it. Some dude started to drop in on her, but she gave a loud whistle, and he broke away. She got a great ride and popped into the air at the end. When she paddled back to the lineup, the guy apologized. She smiled and nodded at him, correctly inferring what he said from his body language. He probably would have tried to chat her up, but it looked like she was out with her boyfriend.

I missed two waves, not having the technique of my twin, but got my groove back on the third and started getting excellent rides. Carly and I shared one, and I felt our special bond coming back. It didn't get much better than that.

When my arms started feeling like cooked macaroni, I said to her, "Let's talk."

We paddled out past where the waves were breaking and sat close together on our boards.

"Carly, I'm still sorry about what happened." I couldn't bring myself to use Patricia's name. "You know that. I hope this thing can bring us together again."

"I don't blame you."

"You don't?"

"Of course not," she said.

"But you wouldn't communicate with me. You ignored my texts and emails."

"Too painful." The sign for "pain" involves the two index fingers pointing at one another and then twisting as if screwing them together. She held her hands close to her heart; that's where it hurt. ASL involves facial expressions as well, and Carly's contorted features showed me the depth of her pain.

We sat for a few minutes watching the blowing fog as it began to clear. I wanted to just hang with her, helping our relationship heal, but I had some business to discuss. I splashed her to get her attention, just as I had done when we surfed together as teenagers.

"Did you go near the Tepona Point trail on your way back from Clam Beach?"

"Why?"

"Just answer the question, Carly."

She looked out to sea for a while. "I may have. It's on the way."

Aargh! I banged my fist against my board. "You didn't think maybe that was something you should have told me?"

"It didn't matter. I didn't push Angelo off the cliff. Why does it matter?"

"Because someone might have seen you near there."

"I doubt it." Her shrug said that it was totally unimportant.

"The police may have a witness who saw you there."

She glanced toward the incoming swells.

"Carly, you can't lie to me. I need to know everything you know."

"That's not what you said in your office." She fingerspelled "subornation of perjury" almost too fast for me to follow. She wore a satisfied smile.

I reached down and splashed some water on my face. Could she have done it? No. I didn't believe it for a second. Did I?

When I looked up, she was paddling toward a wave that towered above its peers. It was going to break outside of the rock. I would have to haul ass to get over it before it broke, so I started after her. It looked like she was aiming to ride it. I put every ounce of my waning strength into my strokes, but things didn't look good.

It was one of those sneaker waves—the kind that knocks tourists off the Redwood Point jetty once a year or so. Carly outpaced me, and as the wave came around the point, she turned and burned. She caught the wave at the perfect spot and crossed along it in front of me. The dudes farther in whooped and whistled, appreciating her performance.

I couldn't have been in a worse location. If I stayed where I was, the tsunami would break right on me. Instead, I called on my forty-three-year-old muscles to earn their keep and get me over the top before it broke. The wave began feathering. I put my head down and kept paddling. Up and up. I was going to make it.

Something grabbed my board. The word "shark" jumped into my head, but it was probably only a length of kelp that got tangled in my leash. It was just enough to kill my effort, and I got that sickening feeling of going over backwards. Over the falls. I rag dolled it, letting the Pacific Ocean do with me what it would. My time to breathe would come again; I just had to wait it out. Unfortunately, my gargantuan effort to beat the wave left me with no oxygen to spare.

There was no way of knowing which way was up. It was as if I were in an underwater tornado. Time dragged on. My longboard was in there with me, along with its razor-sharp fin, but my only concern was getting air. I reached my limit then exceeded it, my brain yelling for me to breathe. In my dark time, I might have yielded, welcoming the chance to die. I might have breathed in the salt water.

That's when the Pacific took pity on me. My arm found itself in the air, and I struggled to the surface, taking in some water with my first desperate breath. I pulled my board to me with the leash and after a quick glance to check that no more waves were coming, draped my arms over it and coughed in more life-giving air.

Carly was by my side in seconds. "Welcome back."

The fog had lifted, and I looked north. Tepona Point stood out clearly. If I were looking at the right time, I'd easily notice a body falling off the cliff.

"Still alive?" Carly signed, smiling.

I pulled myself up onto my board and replied, "No."

An air horn sounded. Up on the cliff above the surf spot, someone was waving both arms. Someone else was doing the same on the beach. I pointed.

Carly looked. "Toby. And Nicole," she said. Toby was my twenty-year-old son.

What could they want? We waved back and paddled in. Carly caught one more wave on the way, so she beat me to the beach.

Conclusive Evidence

As I waded out of the ocean and pulled the leash off my ankle, she signed, "Angelo's body."

Chapter Three

THE DAY AFTER ANGELO'S body was discovered, Louella walked down the ramp to the floating dock at the Woodley Island Marina. It was a cold and damp morning, a typical December day on the North Coast. Seagulls fought over the fish scraps that a fisherman was tossing into the harbor. Barking sea lions got in on the free food. She lit a cigarette and walked to Wenzel Rozetti's boat. Rozetti was the crabber who had encountered the body out on the ocean. The police had blocked the boat off by stringing crime scene tape between traffic cones on the dock. The tape flapped in the wind.

Commercial crabbing season had finally opened following the usual negotiations between canners and fishermen. Amateur crabbers could go out anytime, however, and Rozetti's boat was about as small as they came. All aluminum, it had a 90-horsepower outboard on the back and the standard crane and winch for bringing up the crab pots. Louella took a drag on her cigarette. *Just a hobby for him.*

She wrapped her coat tighter and headed back to her car, a ten-year-old Corolla. She drove ten minutes to Rozetti's house in an area of town where petty crimes and drug busts were common. The bungalow's paint was peeling, and green mold had taken hold on the north wall.

Rozetti answered the door shirtless. A musty heat flowed from the interior while he stood in the doorway. He was a roly-poly fellow, his stomach hanging out over his sweatpants. His face was round, and he hadn't shaved.

"Mr. Rozetti?"

"Yeah?"

"I'd like to ask you some questions about what happened yesterday."

"Who are you?"

"I'm a detective." She pulled out her private investigator license, which didn't look much different from a driver's license.

"I talked to the police yesterday. I told them everything."

"May I come in?" she asked.

He opened the door, backing away. "Yeah. Have a seat. I'm gonna put a shirt on."

Louella looked around the small living room. A flat-screen TV dominated one wall, sitting on a board across two milk crates. A mountain bike with a flat tire leaned against shelves formed with cinder blocks and pressed-wood boards.

Rozetti returned in a sweatshirt and sat across from her in a ratty recliner. "You sure don't look like a detective."

"I'm investigating the disappearance of Angelo Romero. Can you tell me what happened yesterday?" She offered him a cigarette.

He took it and lit up. "It was really weird. I was about a mile out in the ocean."

"Where exactly?"

"Straight out from Redwood Point. So, I see something floating, not too far away. I thought maybe it was a dead seal or something. I motor over there, and I got a bad feeling about it. You know? I got closer, and I saw his face. It was Angelo Romero."

"How did you know?" she asked.

"What do you mean?"

"How did you know it was Angelo Romero?"

"From his face, of course."

"So you knew him. You recognized his face."

"Oh, I see." Rozetti pulled on his ear. "Well, I'd seen his face on the news, so I put two and two together."

"The body was floating faceup?"

"Yeah."

"What happened next?"

"Well," he said, "my radio wasn't working, so I couldn't call the Coast Guard or nothing. I stayed there, thinking. I knew if I went in and called the cops, they'd never find it. Even if I tied a buoy to it. Besides, the thing was barely floating. Kind of amazing that I saw it at all, you know what I mean?"

Louella waited.

"So, I didn't want to do it, but I figure it's my civic duty or whatever. I decide to try and pull it into the boat. I get the boat hook out and snag it by some clothing, but that comes apart. I hook it by the mouth, but the cheek breaks." Rozetti gagged and ran out of the room. Retching noises were followed by the sound of the toilet flushing.

He came back and sat. "Damn. I thought I was done with the puking. Where was I?"

"You had trouble hooking the body."

"Right. So then, the body flips onto its front, facedown, okay? Then it looks like it's going to sink. Like, right away. Maybe moving it around let air out or something. I grab for it again, and it was gross, but I got it hooked under the arm."

He shuddered then continued. "I puked over the side of the boat but hung on. I knew I'd never get it over the gunwale, but I thought maybe I could tie it alongside. Then, the body really starts to sink, and I'm holding the damn thing up with my boat hook. Then I guess the skin ripped or something, because the boat hook comes up, and the body's gone. I motored in and called the police. After I talked to them, they told me it was probably Romero's body."

"Did they say why they thought so?"

"Oh, I forgot. He had a tattoo. On the back of his neck. I told them about that, and they nodded. They must have known about it."

Louella made a note on her pad. "Can you describe it for me?"

"Yeah. It was real colorful. It wasn't big. It was a shark with blood around it."

"What happened then?"

"The police talked to me for a while. They strung up crime scene tape. They put a plastic bag over the tip of the boat hook. Took that away with them. Then they had me come down to the station."

Louella stood. "Thank you, Mr. Rozetti. Here's my card. Please call me if you think of anything else." Louella got to the door and turned. "By the way, what's your day job? When you're not crabbing?"

"Oh, I'm kinda unemployed. But sometimes I work out at the call center."

"Call center?"

"It's called DialUSA. Out in Blue Lake." Blue Lake was a small village twenty miles from Redwood Point.

Louella walked to her car. She got in and paged through her notes. *There.* Romero had some connection with that same call center.

She lit a cigarette and thought for a while then drove away.

I had some time to think while waiting for the settlement conference for the case of the not-so-artificial insemination. I sat by the fire in my office, sipping coffee. *Could Carly and I ever recapture the bond we used to have?* I thought back to the two seismic events that had almost destroyed me. The second one shattered my relationship with Carly.

I had met my wife, Raquel, in court. I was a sophomore in college on a field trip for my Law, Society, and Justice course. She was a newly minted court reporter. As soon as I saw her, the entire court proceeding turned into a droning in the background. It wasn't just her beauty, but her calm competence, recording every word that was said. Perhaps she felt my gaze, because she glanced up at me. We locked eyes but only for a split second. One of my classmates, a cute redhead that I had, until that moment, been pursuing, poked me in the ribs. *Was my infatuation so obvious?*

A Latin beauty, Raquel had a sultry look that reminded me of Salma Hayek or Penelope Cruz. She was an artist's study in shades of brown. Light brown skin, dark brown hair, and eyes bordering on black. I'd never been a fan of the messy hair look. Until then.

During a court recess, she headed down the hall, and I ditched my class and followed. I caught up with her, admiring her hair from behind.

"Sorry for that," I called out. "I was trying not to stare."

She stopped. Turned. "You were staring? Do I know you?" She had a deep voice with the barest hint of a Mexican accent. Could someone not born to English really become a court reporter?

"I wasn't really staring." I was.

She resumed walking. "I didn't notice. Are you on a high school field trip?"

"Ha ha." I hoped she was joking, and I fell into step beside her. "No, I was just curious about your hair. How you get it to look like that."

"Like what?"

"You know. Stylishly messy."

"Huh. Messy."

"In a good way," I said.

"Maybe I just didn't get a chance to comb it today."

We pushed through the doors to the outside. She sat down on the bench by the sidewalk and tilted her face to catch the rays of the sun.

I sat beside her. "Yeah. That's probably it."

"Shouldn't you be with the rest of your class?" She pointed. "There's a playground down the street."

Her tone had turned flirtatious, and my budding eloquence fled like a scared puppy, leaving behind the awkward teenager that I was. I instantly had a new appreciation for the term "tongue-tied." Perhaps when we got close, her sexual magnetism degaussed my brain cells.

"No, I—"

She turned to me. "Maybe I'm a busy person. No time for personal hygiene."

"No, I think … I mean, the rest of you, is, uh …"

"It's only my hair that says homeless person?"

"No, uh, jeez." *Was I really starting to stammer?* Drooling would be next.

"Okay, you got me," she said.

"What?"

She patted her hair. "There's a product I use to make it look like this."

"Oh, really? I see." I crossed my arms. "What's it called?"

"Uh … Sloppy Locks."

"Not Bed Hair and Beyond?"

The corners of her lips twitched up into a smile. A small one that suddenly grew. "I know what hair product you use." She reached up and patted my head, her touch electric. At that point, I still had a full head of curly hair.

"What product would that be?" I asked.

She leaned toward me with a big smile. "I Can't Believe It's Not Better!"

Our courtship was a maelstrom of ups and downs due to her Latin temper and my youth. She and Carly became fast friends. We married only a year after the hair product discussion. Our marriage was even more turbulent than our courtship, but we never stopped loving each other.

The last time I saw her we'd had a vicious argument. I don't remember what it was about. She'd stormed off to a class reunion with her girlfriends from stenography school, slamming the door on the way out. I phoned her to apologize, and when she didn't answer I figured she was still angry. I texted her that I was sorry but got no response.

The return call I eventually received was not from Raquel but from the California Highway Patrol. She'd been killed in a rollover accident. The other driver was drunk.

Carly, nine months pregnant and ready to burst, helped me most with my grief, sitting with me in silence for hours at a time. Our exceptional bond grew even stronger during the ordeal. She tried to distract me by involving me in the preparations for my soon-to-arrive niece. It didn't work. That is, not until the day Patricia was born.

Carly insisted that I be there when she gave birth. Some of her friends thought it was weird, but she didn't care. Angelo happened to be out of town when the time came, so it was just Carly, Nicole, me, the obstetrician, and a nurse in the delivery room.

I'm not one for spiritual thoughts, but the juxtaposition of Raquel leaving the world and Patricia entering it seemed somehow magical. I'm not saying there was any kind of reincarnation involved, but the event seemed outside of the normal, everyday world. I felt an immediate connection with this squally, pinkish-purple bundle. After Carly held her, she handed Patricia to me. Most of the tears shed in the delivery room were mine.

Patricia was deaf. Knowing the possibility of having a deaf child, Angelo had wanted to adopt, but Carly won him over to her way of thinking. She simply didn't see deafness as a disability.

My niece began babbling in sign language as early as seven months of age—making incoherent hand and arm movements that mimicked ours. I'm proud to say that the first sign she produced herself was for "uncle," the letter "U" moved in a circle near her forehead. At least that's what I saw.

She was the darling of the extended family, with spunk and charm that was off the charts. She even made jokes, something that I had been sure was beyond the capability of a toddler. For example, she'd point to something, make the wrong sign, and watch everyone's reactions. She'd point to the picture of the dog in her book, and sign "cat" or "cereal." She knew exactly what she was doing.

A cloud appeared on the horizon when the subject of a cochlear implant came up. When I sensed Carly's resistance, I did my homework and became somewhat of an expert on the topic.

Cochlear implants are, at the same time, an inspired scientific advance and a crude tool. By sliding a tiny electrode array into the snail-like cochlea of the inner ear—it's about the size of a pea—sound waves can be used to directly stimulate the auditory nerve in the different locations along its length that correspond to different frequencies. Thus, the implant bypasses the defective hair cells in the cochlea.

They are crude because humans have 30,000 fibers in the auditory nerve, whereas the array has only about twenty electrodes. However, using electrical wizardry that I don't understand, that's enough for understanding speech—the primary goal. But a CI won't let someone hear the world the way hearing people do.

Carly didn't want Patricia to get a CI, and her view was opposed by our entire extended family. I was the designated persuader-in-chief because of our closeness and because arguing was my profession.

"I like the way I am," Carly said during one of our heated discussions. "Deafness isn't something that needs to be fixed."

"So why do you wear contact lenses?" I replied.

"That's different."

"How?"

"I need contacts to see traffic signs. I don't need to hear to interact with my friends, with my culture. ASL is not an inferior language; it's just different."

It really came down to the special Deaf culture that Carly loved. Capital D. It was Carly's tribe, and I suspected Carly was afraid that Patricia wouldn't learn to sign, that she wouldn't join the tribe.

I frowned. "What about me? I can hear, but I sign. Pretty well, too."

"Some kids hate the CIs. They reject using them." She was just grasping for rationalizations now.

"Okay, if she doesn't like it, fine. She doesn't have to use it."

Carly's face was flushed. "I don't want to make the decision for Patricia. She can decide for herself later on."

"Come on, you know the problem with that."

CIs work best when implanted early on. The ideal age seems to be around eighteen months. Some adults who get an implant have trouble interpreting the unfamiliar impulses that are sent to their brains. Also, CIs provide what's called "phonological awareness" that helps kids read. It helps them sound out words.

I hugged my twin sister, wishing I could talk to her with my arms around her.

I released the hug. "The CI won't make you lose your daughter. You'll see. She already signs better than any kid her age. She has a wonderful, signing family. I'll personally guarantee she's the best signer in Redwood Point. You know she's going to love you no matter what."

Carly had eventually relented and gave up the fight against overwhelming resistance. Patricia would get an implant.

Patricia had had a grand send-off for her surgery, with four grandparents, my immediate family of three, and some of Carly's friends from the deaf community. She was a year and a half old, and Carly and Angelo had prepared her well, going through picture books about visits to the hospital.

The surgery would take three to four hours, so the entire group headed to the hospital cafeteria for a spirited breakfast. Nicole took on the duties of translator for those who didn't sign. Back in the waiting room, we all shared the feeling of supporting Patricia and looked forward to waving to her when she woke up. Since the doctors had assured us that the surgery was a "safe and well-tolerated procedure," our only worry was whether the implantation would be successful.

I looked forward to that moment, three to six weeks after surgery, when the implant would be turned on for the first time. I'd watched many videos of children hearing their first sounds when the device was activated. The payoff was seeing the child suddenly look around when the first tones were transmitted to the device. I was sure that Patricia, being so advanced, would use her sign language skills to communicate how she felt.

I pulled Carly aside and asked, "How are you doing?"

She shrugged. She was handling the situation with good grace, accepting the will of the "village" that was our extended family. I resisted the urge to repeat my arguments. The pros and cons had been hashed over enough.

An hour in, I walked over to the doors to the surgery department. I saw some frantic comings and goings for the OR that held my niece. An icicle of worry invaded my heart.

Soon after that, the head surgeon walked to the waiting room, his head down. He asked to speak privately with Carly and Angelo.

Chapter Four

IN MY OFFICE, NICOLE put her hand on my shoulder, startling me out of my agonizing revisitation of those events.

"You okay, Dad?" she asked.

"What? Oh, sorry. Yeah, I'm fine."

"They just arrived. Horace Scully, Molly Scully, and Molly's attorney. You're sure you're okay?"

"Yeah, just enjoying the fire. Show them in."

Ursula Pinart, Molly's lawyer, came in first and gave me a peck on the cheek. A little more than a peck, actually. She was a good friend and a competent attorney. Ursula was a few years older than I, with salt-and-pepper hair pulled back into a tight bun. She looked more like a psychological counselor than a legal one, with a smile that radiated kindness and eyes that twinkled, as if she were about to share a joke.

Molly followed with a bit of a limp and an apologetic grimace. "I'm so sorry, Ursula said it would be okay to bring her." She had her daughter on her hip, a cute pixie whose pigtails were tied with pink bows.

"You must be Hortense," I said, leaning down. "How old are you, Hortense?"

She turned away, squeezing her head against her mom's shoulder, but held up a hand with four fingers awkwardly extended.

"Four years old. What a big girl!" That was how old Patricia would have been. I blinked a few times. *Keep it together, Garrett.*

"She's shy, and she'll be quiet. She's very well behaved."

Nicole was behind Horace. "Dad, I'd be happy to watch her—"

I made the sign for "No!" and said out loud, "Why don't you get some coffees?"

She took the orders, and I got the clients seated around the table in the center of my office. I kept a box of toys by the fireplace.

"Hortense, you're welcome to play with any of these. This one on the top is a lot of fun." The centerpiece of my kid zone was a six-sided play cube with a bead maze on the top—colorful wires with beads that could be moved along them. Each side had fun activities such as interlocking plastic gears and an abacus.

Hortense shook her head and gripped her mom tighter.

"Or not. But feel free to play with them if you get bored." I returned to the table, a heavy antique that matched the men's club atmosphere.

"Pleased to meet you, Molly. I'm very sorry for your loss." I shook her hand. She was apparently fighting a battle against her weight, a war the bad guys were winning, but her round face was pleasant and held a warm smile.

"Horace, good to see you again." I shook his hand, having trouble reading his mood. He wore the same maroon suit jacket as before.

Ursula said, "Why don't you get things started, Garrett?"

"Okay." I sat. "Ursula and I have gone over things, and I hope we've found a solution that you can all be happy with. First, let me tell you what I've discovered. I learned that although the chances are slight, there is a chance that ..." I had to choose language that would pass over Hortense's head. "... that the paternity doesn't belong to Horace. It's unlikely, but possible, that Keith is the, uh, *padre*. Are you all understanding?"

Molly tensed, and Ursula put her hand on Molly's arm.

"I've found that it would be possible to determine paternity through a DNA test. Even though Keith and Horace were identical twins, it turns out that there would be differences in their DNA. Differences that would be few and far between. The process for finding them is something like working out the entire genome or something. I don't really understand the details, but it's a big deal. A regular paternity test costs a few hundred dollars. I couldn't pin down the full cost from the geneticist I spoke with, but I got the impression it could be quite high. I can't imagine that you'd want to pay for the full DNA sequencing, Horace, which is unlikely to give you the result you want."

While I was talking, Hortense climbed down from her mom's lap. But instead of going over to the toys, she went around the table and climbed into the lap of the man who was probably her father. Seeing the surprise on Molly's face, I concluded that she hadn't coached the child to do that. Ursula gave me a discreet wink.

I kept blabbing away about the DNA test, while from the corner of my eye I watched the delicate scene being played out on Horace's side of the table. Hortense pulled herself up and whispered in her dad's ear then pointed to one of the bows in her hair. She had brown, captivating eyes that reminded me of the kids in those black-velvet paintings.

I finished my lecture and said, "Ursula, why don't you talk about Molly's finances?"

"Right." She consulted her notes. "Molly is currently in debt to the tune of twelve thousand dollars, and she's behind on her—"

Horace sat up straighter. "If she hadn't spent—"

It was my turn to put a restraining hand on my client's arm. Hortense shifted on his lap then relaxed again.

Ursula continued, "She's behind on her rent. Keith and Molly had a good nest egg going, by today's standards, but the surgery on her leg wasn't covered by her health insurance due to a technical issue. That ate up their savings—her savings—and she was forced to take out a loan. We're going after the health insurance company, but that will take time."

"You didn't have life insurance?" Horace asked. It was the first interaction he'd had with his sister-in-law. He now had his arm around Hortense, and she seemed to be asleep, her thumb in her mouth.

Molly shook her head. "Keith and I had talked about it. I thought he'd bought it. He handled all the financial stuff. After he was gone, I found that he hadn't. He had all the paperwork ready to go, but he hadn't sent it in." She took a breath with a little catch in it. "Horace, I never would have come to you, but I'm really stuck here."

I let the revelations sink in, then I brought up the settlement Ursula and I had devised.

"Horace, I understand how you hate recurring expenses, so we've structured a one-time lump-sum payment that will let Molly escape the financial hole she's in. Through no fault of her own, I'd like to stress. I can assure you, Horace, that the courts won't look favorably on your unconventional, or maybe I should say conventional, insemination technique."

Both Horace and Molly blushed so intensely that the heat from their faces might have raised the temperature in the room.

"If you recall," I continued, "Molly had a dental hygienist license. That expired, but I've learned that she should have no trouble getting recertified, and my dentist tells me the job opportunities are good around here. Hortense will be in kindergarten next year, making Molly able to work without having to pay for full-time daycare. If Molly's suit against the health insurance carrier is successful—any idea of the chances, Ursula?"

"I'm hopeful, but it's too soon to say. We've retained a good lawyer who specializes in those issues."

"Okay, so we can't count on that, Horace, but if it's successful, Molly would use that settlement to pay you back. We've put strong language in there that makes it clear you've fulfilled any responsibility and that Molly agrees to not come after you for more money in the future. As I've explained, the courts will usually look to the best interests of the child in these situations, but we've done the best we can."

I put two copies of the agreement on the table, circled the lump-sum total, and slid one to each of the parents. Horace stiffened when he saw the total, but my chief negotiator, the one on his lap, was working her magic. Molly and Horace agreed to think about it and left.

Ursula stayed behind. "You are one sneaky guy. That was pretty risky, wasn't it? If the girl had had a temper tantrum, it would have backfired."

I smiled. "Yes. But you told me how cute and well-behaved Hortense was. I sure didn't expect her to go over and sit in his lap. That was a bonus."

We both laughed.

"Would you like a drink to celebrate?" I asked.

"It's not settled yet."

"Oh, I think Horace's iceberg of a heart has undergone some global warming."

I pulled a bottle and two tumblers from a cabinet and poured a little Green Spot Whiskey into each. We clinked glasses, and I put another log on the fire. We talked about old times, and I told her about what was happening with Carly. Before she left, she gave me a hug and another warm kiss on the cheek.

After she was gone, Nicole said, "You know she has the hots for you, right, Dad?"

"Who, Ursula? Oh, no, she's just a good friend."

"You are so clueless sometimes. And I would have been happy to watch the little girl while you guys were in there."

I savored the warmth of the whiskey. "She was sweet, wasn't she?"

Patricia's death had thrown me into a spiral of grief. An explosive device filled with heartache and anguish had gone off in the center of Patricia's extended family, leaving no one standing. As expected, Carly was hit the hardest. When the surgeon gave her the news that Patricia had died on the table, she went catatonic. He admitted her to the hospital, shooting her full of industrial-strength sedatives.

The saddest words in the English language are "if only." In my brain, I knew I didn't bear the blame for my niece's death, but I couldn't convince my heart of that. If only I hadn't used my professionally tuned persuasive skills to push Carly over to the family's way of thinking, our beautiful and extraordinary angel would still be alive. Patricia didn't need that damned device in her head to be happy. She would have thrived in the deaf community, spreading her special talent for joy throughout Redwood Point. Sure, my reasoning was faulty, but I couldn't force myself to view things objectively.

After six months, I found myself stalled in the third stage of grief: depression. In fact, I suspected that I was dealing with something more than grief. It seemed to me that the shock of Patricia's death had awakened an underlying condition, like arousing a sleeping dragon. I'd been able to survive those six months only by devoting myself to the negligence lawsuit against the hospital and the anesthesiologist.

The procedure was a safe one, but the doctor in charge of keeping my niece alive and free from pain had dozed off. When the machine feeding Patricia oxygen malfunctioned, the sleeping doctor, who had partied hard the night before and who still had alcohol in his bloodstream, failed to notice. I negotiated a nine-million-dollar settlement, but Carly refused to touch the funds. "Blood money" she called it, donating every penny to Bizet University. Angelo was too traumatized to object. I refused my cut of the settlement, of course.

My depression grew worse once the negotiations were completed. The distraction had held the demons at bay, and once released, they attacked my sanity, dragging me down into a black hole of despair. My work no longer seemed worthwhile—most of my clients were guilty as hell and deserved to be locked up. Jen took over my active cases, and I refused all new clients.

The things I'd enjoyed in the past—surfing, reading, chess, even eating—gave me no pleasure. Everyday activities, such as taking a shower, seemed like dreary chores. I was bored. I abandoned every book I started, even favorites that I'd enjoyed in the past. My computer gave me nothing but problems, the car had annoying rattles, people tailgated, dogs barked at night, and nothing worked the way it should.

Some days I tried to be productive. I remember one morning in the office, sitting hunched over with my forehead resting on the edge of the desk.

Jen burst in. "Hey, boss, did you sign the—hey, what's wrong?"

I did a convincing job of pretending I'd dropped something under the desk. I pinched away my tears and managed a little laugh. "Nothing's wrong. I just dropped something."

Whenever the local news reported that someone had been killed in an accident, my immediate thought was, *Lucky guy.* Sure, I was aware that my thought processes were out of whack, but I couldn't do anything about it.

My dead wife appeared to me in my dreams. She never said anything, but I saw it in her look: *Snap out of it, Garrett!*

Insomnia wormed its way into my life, cutting off the relief that unconsciousness might have given me. I followed all the advice on the internet trying to shake it. No luck. I would fall asleep fine but wake after only a few hours and spend the rest of my night fending off toxic thoughts. It was the insomnia that led me to seek help from my doctor, a woman who looked too young to be practicing medicine yet made up for her inexperience with an encyclopedic knowledge of physiology and an exceptional mind. Despite a busy schedule, she always gave me her full attention and never made me feel rushed.

I sat on the edge of the exam table in a room filled with the scent of rubbing alcohol and described my problem with sleeping.

When I was done, she asked the question I was dreading: "Are you depressed?"

I looked her in the eye. "No."

It hurt me to lie, but I had to deny it. An essential skill for a lawyer, as for a chess player, is the ability to think through a chain of events that would follow any move or response. If I move my pawn here, she'll move her knight there, and so on. In my mind, I predicted that the entire conversation would go in a direction I didn't want:

Doctor: Are you depressed?

Me: Yes.

Doctor: Do you have thoughts of harming yourself?

Me: Almost every day. I get great comfort from imagining killing myself. Lying in bed at night, I go over the different ways to do it.

Doctor: Does that scare you?

Me: Not at all. Death would be a wonderful escape from the pain.

Doctor: What about your children?

Me: They're grown. They'd get over it. I'm not even sure they love me. In this state I'm probably a burden to them.

Doctor: You don't really believe that, do you?

Me: Shrug.

Doctor: Garrett, I know I can help you. Return you to a life that includes joy and contentment. Until then, can you promise me something?

Me: I know what you're going to say.

Doctor: Can you promise me you won't do anything drastic? You won't harm yourself?

Me: What value would a promise like that hold? I mean, once I'm dead … and besides, I could never give up my one means of escape.

At that point, the doctor would press a button under her desk, and two burly men in white coats would come and take me to the loony ward for a seventy-two-hour hold. Worse, I would be subjected to years of therapy sessions, which, to an introvert like me, would be a fate worse than death. So I lied to my doctor, and based on my incomplete information, she prescribed some remedies that failed to make a dent in my insomnia. For example, Ambien knocked me out quickly but only for only two hours at a time.

A few weeks later, I decided to come clean. I returned to my doctor's office. When she came in, I took a deep breath and made the plunge.

"I lied to you," I said.

"About the depression?"

"Yes. You knew?"

"I suspected it."

The surprise was that we didn't go down the dreaded conversational path I'd imagined. I don't know if it was a "don't ask, don't tell" policy or something else, but instead of inquiring about the depth of my despair, she prescribed an antidepressant that had a useful side effect: sedation.

It didn't keep me asleep all night, but with some experimentation I found a system that worked for me. When I woke around two a.m., as I invariably did, I took the pill the doc prescribed. That always sent me back to la la land and kept me there until it was time to get up.

I wasn't magically returned to psychic health, but one morning, when I woke refreshed and rebooted, I knew I'd reached a turning point. It's hard to overstate the value of being unconscious for eight or even nine hours. No matter what happened during the day, I could always escape into oblivion at night and rise in the morning to a clean slate.

My text alert broke through the cobwebs of my sleeping-pill-influenced brain. Five after six in the morning.

Carly had texted, *They want to search my house. Can they do that?*

I massaged my face and replied, *Don't interfere. Don't answer ANY questions. I'm coming.*

I dragged myself to the guest room door and banged on it. "Nicole, I need your help. Can you get dressed quickly, please?"

I'd taken the sleeping pill only a few hours earlier. Getting stopped for driving under the influence wouldn't help things. No time for coffee, I downed a caffeine pill and ran the shaver over my face. My wonderful daughter appeared wearing jeans, t-shirt, and a questioning look.

"I have to go to Aunt Patricia's right away. I'm too sleepy to drive. Can you take me there?"

She squinted and cocked her head. "You said, 'Aunt Patricia'!"

"Aunt Carly's. Sorry."

On the way over, Nicole asked, "The police don't have to wait until you get there?"

"No. You should know that."

"Hey, it's pretty early in the morning."

"I'm sorry, sweetheart. I just want to make sure they don't try to ask Carly anything."

Nicole took the Westhaven exit. "She knows, Dad."

"I wouldn't put it past Crawford to try to trick her into saying something."

Carly's house sat on Scenic Drive, only a little north of Tepona Point. Years ago, she'd had a spectacular view of the ocean, but the trees had grown and blocked much of it. It was still a wonderful place to live. The entrance had a small portico with benches on each side of the front door. As we came up the driveway, Carly was sitting on one of those benches. Next to her was my twenty-year-old son, Toby.

"What's he doing here?" I said to Nicole.

"Don't ask me."

There was one squad car and an unmarked in the driveway. Nicole parked where she wouldn't block them in. On the porch I gave Toby a hug. "How you doing, buddy?"

He responded with a shrug.

"I have to talk confidentially with your aunt Carly now. I want to visit with you later, okay?"

He wandered off, giving us privacy.

I asked Carly, "All good?"

She nodded, looking unreasonably calm.

"Show me the search warrant."

It was standard and correct, stating "… that there is probable cause to believe that the property and/or person described herein may be found at the locations set forth herein and is lawfully seizable pursuant to Penal Code Section 1524 as indicated below by 'x' …" The "x" was next to "it tends to show that a felony has been committed." The list included any and all of Carly's computers and smartphones. In other words, this was a fishing expedition. More worrisome was the item, "Any and all clothing with the Bizet University logo."

"Anything I should know about on your computers?"

"Nothing."

I took a breath, relaxing for the first time since the phone woke me. I looked at my two kids talking.

Carly tapped me on the shoulder. "Except …"

Oh, crap.

"There are some searches that could be problematic," she explained.

I made the sign for "fuck." It looks like two bunnies bumping uglies.

After thinking for a while, I said, "I think we can deal with that. Do you have cloud backup?"

"Yes." She took my pad again and wrote down *TrueImageBackup.com* and the password for it. She gave me the information I needed to access her password manager also.

"Excellent. I'll get it all restored to another Mac, and we'll be able to see what they can see."

A middle-aged woman with a badge on her belt but no uniform came over and squatted down in front of Carly. "I'm going to bring your MacBook Pro and your iPhone over and ask that you unlock them with your fingerprint." The ASL interpreter translated.

"Do I have to do that?" Carly asked me.

"Yes, you do." Passwords are protected under the Fifth Amendment to the Constitution. They are things that you know, and the amendment states that no person "shall be compelled in any criminal case to be a witness against himself." Fingerprints are not things that you know; they are physical things. They aren't covered. In the same way, the police can force you to hand over a key to a locked safe but can't make you tell them the combination. Laws don't always make sense.

I called a tech guy I'd had on retainer in the past—someone I'd trust with my life. He answered on the third ring. *Yes!* I stepped away from prying ears and told him what I wanted. With the rush-demand pricing, he said he could reproduce her MacBook by early afternoon. I gave him the passwords.

After another thirty minutes, the police finished up and handed her a receipt for the items taken. She and I both signed it. The police drove away.

Inside, I was impressed that they hadn't torn the place apart. Carly joked that it was neater than when they'd come.

Toby and Nicole joined us, and Carly fixed breakfast. The country-style kitchen was the best room in the house, with a wrought iron chandelier hanging from the rough beams of the ceiling. I cracked one window to let in the chatter of the nearby brook. It was a sound Carly would never be able to appreciate. The aroma of the frying bacon, however, was something we could all enjoy.

My son had a short, scraggly beard and a faint mustache. Raquel and I had always worried about him because, unlike Nicole, his personality was a bit off-center. He'd exhibited dramatic mood swings from the moment he was born, though he attempted to hide them as he grew older. He had strange ideas about how the world worked and was rarely comfortable around others, even family.

It turned out we shouldn't have worried. He found his niche in nature photography and, against all odds, seemed able to eke out a living at it.

I finished off a perfect piece of bacon and turned to him. "I was surprised to see you here, Toby. What's up?"

He started with spoken English, but quickly realized his mistake and switched to sign. "Oh, I don't know. I just thought Aunt Carly could use some love and support. You know."

I glanced at Carly, but she was busy with the pancakes and hadn't noticed the conversation.

"I'm sure she appreciates that," I said. "How's business?"

"Oh, it's okay. I sold a photo to a guy in New York."

"Nice."

Toby had moved out when he graduated high school but still lived nearby.

We all caught up with each other, ignoring for a time the worsening situation with the police.

While Nicole and Toby cleaned up, Carly took me into another room and closed the door. If you want to have a private conversation in ASL, distance alone doesn't do the trick.

"I'm worried about Toby," she said.

"What do you mean? What happened?"

"He showed up here at two in the morning. I'd gotten up to go the bathroom, and I saw a light on in the living room. I grabbed a baseball bat and went to look, and he was there."

I frowned and cocked my head. "Toby was in the living room?"

"He was going through the books on the shelves. I watched for a minute. He'd take one out, page through it, and put it back. I flashed the lights and he jumped."

"You don't lock your door?"

She shook her head. "No one around here does."

"What did he say?"

"Said he was looking for some passage he remembered. It was the inspiration for a photo. Or something. He was signing so fast, I could hardly keep up."

Carly couldn't keep up? Impossible. "Okay, thanks for telling me. You've got enough on your plate; I don't want you to have to worry about it. I'll deal with it."

Chapter Five

BY MERE CHANCE, I was present when the police arrested Carly on the campus of Bizet University. We were there for a roundtable discussion about Bizet's relationship to the community of Redwood Point. With the goal of getting reacquainted with my sister, I accepted when she'd asked me to attend.

Detective Crawford apparently planned to maximize Carly's embarrassment. I could see no reason for it beyond a petty desire for revenge. If so, he'd misestimated my sister. Her face flushed only slightly. She kept her anger hidden. We'd discussed the possibility of arrest, and I'd advised Carly about what would happen, but it still took me by surprise. *Did they find something on her computer?*

"There's no need to handcuff her," I told the detective. Someone in the group translated my words to ASL. Handcuffing her was equivalent to putting duct tape over her mouth.

"Standard procedure," he replied.

The uniformed cop snapped the cuffs on her wrists.

Carly was well respected in the community, and the way she was being treated led to some yelling among the vocal members of the group.

She turned around and fingerspelled, "It's okay." It was the first time I'd had to read fingerspelling upside down.

Crawford had brought an interpreter, something required by law because the arrest had been planned. I walked backwards in front of her, reminding her of the things we'd discussed.

"Don't talk with anyone," I signed.

She gave me a look that said I was an idiot. I explained that they'd take a mug shot, take her property and clothing, fingerprint her, conduct a full-body search, and perhaps do some health screening. She was in for a shock, and perhaps knowing what to expect would help.

Her composure broke right as they were putting her into the backseat of the squad car, but she took a deep breath and steeled herself. If anyone could handle this, she could.

In 2015, an appeals court held that lawyers and clients must be able to have physical, face-to-face meetings in jail. I got to the meeting room while Carly was still being processed. After forty minutes she arrived, looking small. The intake procedure had certainly been demeaning, but she was tough. She wore the standard orange pants and top provided to prisoners, and the clothing was surprisingly dirty. A closer look suggested they had been recently laundered but that the grime was too entrenched. They were permanently dirty.

As soon as they removed her cuffs, she said, "Get me out of here."

I've mentioned that Carly doesn't suffer fools gladly, and unfortunately many low-level civil servants fall into that category. Some deputies were assigned to work in the jail because they lacked the social skills to interact with the general public. They had no manners.

"Unfortunately, they arrested you late on Friday so that you'll have to stay in jail over the weekend. It sucks and it's unfair. It's Crawford's doing, but we're stuck with it. I'm sorry, sis. At least they didn't arrest you on Christmas Eve." The date was December 28.

"They put me in a cell with an inmate who is deaf and who signs. I don't know her, however—"

"No!"

"No, what?"

"Did you talk with her?"

"A little."

"I told you not to speak with anyone. Not a word. Maybe I wasn't clear. Did you think they put her in with you to be nice?"

Carly said nothing.

"What did you talk about?" I demanded.

"Nothing to do with the case. Just small talk."

"Like?"

"She's from Southern California. We just talked about the weather, the deaf communities here and there."

I didn't like it. "From now on, don't communicate with her at all. Tell her your lawyer prohibits it. Is that clear?"

* * *

My impossibly young tech consultant brought a new MacBook Air to the office early on Saturday morning.

"This is essentially a clone of Carly's machine," he said, tapping the laptop, "At least as of yesterday morning. She did a full image backup, and I was able to restore it to this."

"Where did you get it?"

"It was mine. It's yours now; I'll buy myself a new one."

I smiled. "And you'll put it on my tab."

"Plus a handling fee, you got it." On his way out, he winked at Jen, who was standing in the doorway to my office.

She came over and gave me a kiss. Smack on the lips.

I jerked my head back. "What the hell was that?"

She pointed up. Apparently, before Christmas someone—*Nicole!*—had taped a sprig of mistletoe to the ceiling over my desk.

I laughed, but Jen just looked at me with her poker face.

I said, "Is it tiring being inscrutable all the time?"

That got a tiny smile from her. I'm not sure where the stereotype of Asians being inscrutable came from, but with Jen, it fit. When she wanted to, she could make her face a mask of neutrality—the visual equivalent of *no comment.*

Twenty-eight years old, Jen's serious expression worked well with her deadpan humor. She uses that to her advantage in the courtroom, detonating the occasional zinger with deadly effect. Also when I need to be knocked down a peg. I'm okay with that.

When she's in the office, she lets her dark hair fall down to her shoulders, tucked behind her ears. In court, she twists it up into some kind of bun. She usually wears jade earrings that look like green pearls. She told me they were handed down from some distant ancestor and have mystical properties. She didn't smile when she said that. More deadpan humor? I couldn't tell, but she's too down-to-earth to believe in anything supernatural.

She has a delightful face, dominated by piercing eyes and little doll lips that carry lipstick only during trials. In her photograph on the Goodlove and Shek website, her eyes follow you around if you move your head. There's no escape.

I'd rescued her from the public defender's office, where she'd carried twice the caseload of anyone else and had the highest acquittal rate in the department's history.

"Pull up a chair," I said. "Let's see what's on her machine."

Jen dragged a chair over from the conference table. "Should we wait until Carly can be here while we look?"

"Nah, she gave me permission."

I started with Carly's browser history, the first place the police would look. I chose History/Show All History from the Firefox menu—I know my way around computers. The browser had recorded over 4,000 sites visited each month.

I started by entering "cliff" into the search bar for the history entries. I held my breath.

"What's your thinking?" Jen asked.

"I'm just starting. If she'd searched for 'how to push someone off a cliff' or 'death by falling off a cliff,' it would be bad." There were no entries like that. I didn't tell Jen that I had researched similar topics myself when depressed.

"Try 'kill,'" Jen suggested.

That made more sense.

Aargh. The top result was "16 steps to kill someone and not get caught."

"I was afraid of that, but we can explain it." I filled Jen in.

"Now, or save it for the trial?"

"Tough question. Let's see what they have at the preliminary hearing."

I visited the site, and one of the sixteen steps was "Don't take your cell phone." I made a note to check whether Carly had her phone with her on the day of Angelo's death. If so, the police would have a full record of exactly where she'd gone and when.

Jen pointed to my note. "You can check that now."

"What do you mean?"

"Here, let me drive." Jen pushed me to the side and typed in "maps.google.com." She brought up the Google menu and chose "Your timeline" then selected the date of the incident.

My jaw dropped. "Wow!"

"What?"

"I had no idea that was going on."

"Big Brother is watching," she said. "You can go back years and see where you went on any given date."

She zoomed the map in and put Tepona Point in the center. "Good news. She was nowhere near Tepona Point."

"But she said she walked from Clam Beach to home. Right by Tepona Point."

"Well, either she lied or she didn't have her phone with her. I'm guessing the latter. I take my phone running, but only because—"

"You listen to music."

"Right." Jen sat back and aimed her laser eyes at me. "So, if she did it, it's lucky she didn't have her phone."

"But if she did have her phone, it could have exonerated her. The case could be dismissed Monday. You think she did it?"

"I said, 'if she did it.'"

That took my mind back to the book ghostwritten for O.J. Simpson: *If I Did It*. I persisted. "But what do you think?"

"Doesn't matter what I think; it only matters what the jury thinks, something yours truly has said many times. You may be getting too personally involved here."

"Abso-freaking-lutely, I'm taking it personally. You should be first chair on this thing, no matter what Carly says. I'm out of practice for criminal defense."

She patted my knee. "We'll do it together, boss. We have complementary skills."

We continued through Carly's browsing history. "How to kill someone and get away with it," "How to commit the perfect murder," "The only murdering guide you'll ever need," and so on.

Crawford would have wet dreams over that.

Chapter Six

LOUELLA MET HER FORMER partner Vince Rolewicz at the Larrupin' Cafe, twenty miles north of town. It was a miracle he'd agreed to meet with her—she was now batting for the opposition. But even if they were seen together, they could just say they were getting together for old times' sake. She'd mentored him for years, from the time he made detective to the day she retired.

Looking like a farm boy—he was, in fact, the son of a dairy farmer—he had a freckled complexion and light brown hair. His teeth were even, at least by Humboldt standards, and a faint scar ran from one side of his mouth to his ear.

They both ordered the barbecued brisket, Louella asking the waiter for the pieces that were so fatty they'd normally be discarded. "The key to my slim figure," she said.

"That and the smoking." Vince raised his beer glass.

"Smoking helps you lose weight, one lung at a time."

"Mark Twain?"

Louella shook her head. "Alfred E. Neuman."

"Who dat?"

"Great scholar. Before your time, Vince. How's the department?"

"Better now."

"Ever since I retired."

He dropped his jaw theatrically. "Huh. Now that you mention it …"

The waiter brought the food, and they dug in, enjoying their meals along with the cozy atmosphere and the soft jazz coming from the speakers in the ceiling.

"So, you're working with Goodlove, huh?" Vince asked. "I thought he went whacko or something."

Louella finished her bite. "For a while. Depression. He's okay now. Any inside dope on the Romero case?"

"Ah, jeez, you know I can't talk about that."

"So you're happy with the way Crawford is handling the case?"

Vince looked out the window.

"He's not getting any better, is he?" Louella said.

"Worse." He turned back to look at her. "Okay, here's the story. He's been wanting to get back at Carly Romero ever since 2011. The protest."

"The guy is famous for his grudges." Louella sipped her wine, thinking about Crawford's history. Seven years earlier, he'd shot an unarmed civilian. His police car's dashcam had recorded most of the incident.

A report had come in concerning a black man in a neighborhood where, according to the caller, "he didn't belong." It was late afternoon. Had it been dark, the incident might have been avoided, since the car's headlights would have announced its presence.

The squad car rolled slowly behind the man. Over the loudspeaker, Crawford ordered him to stop and put up his hands. The man ignored the command. Crawford's partner said he thought the man was carrying a gun, followed by the prescient words, "What, is he deaf or something?"

Unfortunately, the partner's question didn't start the wheels turning in Crawford's head. Redwood Point has an unusually high percentage of deaf residents. Many who graduate from Bizet elect to stay in the area. Once you get a taste of the uncrowded life, it's hard to go back to a big city. Getting out, Crawford again ordered the man to stop. Crawford and the suspect got out of range of the dashcam, but the last words picked up were spoken by the partner: "Hey, maybe he really ..." There was a big argument in the hearing about whether the inaudible words were "is deaf" or "does have a gun." The partner insisted it was the latter, and no one was able to shake him on that.

No more of the interaction appeared on the dashcam, but three shots rang out in the recording. Crawford testified that the man had spun around and seemed ready to bring a gun to bear, but no weapon was ever found, only a larger than normal smartphone.

The civilian died at the scene. It turned out he lived in that neighborhood, renting a house with four other Bizet University students.

The internal investigation, which the public saw as a whitewash, cleared Crawford of wrongdoing, but his advancement to detective was delayed. Carly led a protest over the incident, which went national, and apparently Crawford focused his frustration on her.

The insult that added to his injury came a year later, when he was back on active duty. Crawford was assigned to break up a sit-in, one unrelated to any police misconduct. His vindictive nature led him like a guided missile to Carly. Caught on cell phone video, he sent an orange stream of pepper spray directly into her face. She sat there stoically despite the pain. Crawford then attempted to yank Carly to her feet, but he lost his grip on her sweater. What followed was a hilarious slapstick routine in which he stumbled backwards with windmilling arms. Just when it seemed he'd regain his balance, he tripped over another protester and landed on his butt. It had become a viral YouTube sensation set to the Benny Hill theme song or with a farting noise dubbed over each of his steps and jumps.

"What's so funny?" Vince asked.

"The video."

Vince laughed. "It never gets old, does it?"

If that wasn't bad enough, Crawford saw that his performance was being filmed, and he stormed over to the videographer, demanding her name. The woman knew her rights. Refused to provide it. Crawford gave up only when his supervisor told him to stand down— also caught on the phone's camera.

"You got to hand it to him for sticking around, though." Louella turned her wineglass on the table. "If that had happened to me, I'd have resigned and moved to another state. Or country."

"Yeah, well Crawford's different. My wife says he's a narcissist and a sociopath who can never see anything he does as wrong. The whole incident just stuck in his craw. I'm amazed he made detective. Sometimes I think he has something on the top brass. I do everything I can to stay out of his way, and you probably should, too."

"Maybe," Louella said. "But that's not how I roll."

Much of the Humboldt County Courthouse smelled like marijuana. I'd noticed that even before the drug was made legal. Perhaps defendants needed some help relaxing. In the stairwell to the second floor, heading to Carly's arraignment, I could have used something to take the edge off. I stopped on a landing and sucked in some calming breaths. *It's just an arraignment.* In my former life, before Raquel's and Patricia's deaths, something like this wouldn't have made the slightest dent in my confidence. I argued myself out of my hopelessness and continued up the stairs.

Courtroom 2 was the smallest in the building, used for arraignments and other matters that were unlikely to attract spectators. The courtroom was a lot like one of those small theaters in a multiplex, with seats for no more than twenty or so visitors. It was like being in a shoebox.

The district attorney herself, Sibyl Finn, would be arguing for the People. She was a striking woman, with hair so bright red—orange almost—that it couldn't have come out of a bottle. No company would market such an over-the-top color. Her complexion was a whiter shade of pale. Exposure to the sun would probably kill her, even in foggy Redwood Point. She wore a blue pin-striped pantsuit that was tailor-made for her curvy figure.

We shook hands. We'd worked together when I was a prosecutor, and we'd battled on opposing sides three times—one win, one loss, one tie. Detective Damon Crawford sat right behind her. He fixed his dead-eye stare on me, but I ignored him.

I had successfully argued that even though we weren't in front of a jury, Carly should be allowed to appear in civilian clothes and without handcuffs. We'd chosen her favorite outfit: a white blouse with a black pencil skirt. Anything to make her more comfortable.

"Are you ready to go forward with the arraignment at this time?" Judge Thomas asked.

Unlike many states, California does not have a mandatory retirement age, and Judge Thomas's presence on the bench was a good argument for reevaluating that. He was in his late eighties and always a little slow to respond. I suspected it was due to plaque buildup in his brain rather than a cautious nature.

"We are, Your Honor," I said.

"Do you waive statement of constitutional rights?"

Carly gave the sign for "yes," and the ASL translator spoke the word. She was the best in the county.

Judge Thomas was unprepared for this, apparently. "Can your client speak, Mr. Goodlove?"

Carly tensed, and I put a hand on her shoulder.

"In the interest of clarity, Your Honor, it would better if she replies in American Sign Language, as is her right."

Judge Thomas said, "Ah. I see."

After some more preliminaries, the judge read from his notes, slowly. "You are charged in this complaint, case number CR 2987632, that on or around December third, 2018, you committed the crime of first-degree murder in violation of Penal Code Section one eight seven in that you did willfully and unlawfully and with malice aforethought murder Angelo Romero. It is further alleged that in commission of that offense, you lay in wait for the victim."

The judge looked up. "Ms. Romero, do you understand the charges as I have read them to you?"

"Yes, Your Honor."

"And have you discussed these charges with your lawyer?"

"Yes, I have."

"At this time do you wish to enter a plea of guilty or not guilty?"

Carly stood straighter. "Not guilty."

The back and forth translations were already becoming automatic.

"At this time," I said, "we would like to request a preliminary hearing in the next ten days as provided by law."

After setting a date within the requested period, Judge Thomas gave the pronouncement I'd expected: "Since this case involves murder with the special circumstance of lying in wait, bail is denied."

"May it please the Court, Your Honor, the prosecution has obviously overfiled in terms of the absurd lying-in-wait allegation. Our understanding is that the charge is based on an eyewitness who we will be able to show is unreliable. In addition, and perhaps more importantly, they have no evidence to put Ms. Romero at the scene before the victim fell off the cliff."

Judge Thomas looked over to the prosecution table. "People?"

"Your Honor, not only will we show that Ms. Romero was at the scene of the crime, but we will have evidence that she planned this murder ahead of time."

"Which, even if true, would not be a special circumstance." I kept my tone relaxed. I've found that yelling or acting excited tends to lessen the gravity of my words. All of my tension and hopelessness was gone at that point.

The judge's eyebrows dropped down toward his eyes like a pair of guillotines. "Do not interrupt, Mr. Goodlove. Perhaps you don't recall how I run my courtroom. I know it's been a while."

I was surprised that he remembered me. Maybe he wasn't senile after all.

He turned his gaze back to Sibyl Finn. "People, do you have any evidence that the defendant was present at the scene before the victim arrived?"

Finn answered, "No, Your Honor, not at this time. But we feel that—"

"Mr. Goodlove, do you have further arguments concerning bail?"

"I do, Your Honor. Ms. Romero has resided in this community since she was a child. She is a well-respected member of the deaf community here, with strong ties to it. She has no history of violence and does not present a danger to public safety."

"People?"

"Ms. Romero does have a prior conviction."

"Are you referring to the trespassing charge?"

"Yes, Your Honor."

"That is barely relevant, Ms. Finn. As you know, that charge was related to a peaceful protest many years ago."

Wow. The judge had done some research.

"Ms. Finn, I agree with Mr. Goodlove that you are attempting to overstate your case, as if you're haggling over a price at a flea market. I am eliminating the special circumstances charge, and bail will be set at one million dollars. Is that acceptable, Mr. Goodlove?"

"It is, Your Honor. Thank you."

Judge Thomas rapped his gavel.

"Now what happens?" Carly signed.

I pointed to the screen of my notebook computer and started typing. "I forgot to mention we won't sign while we're in public. Too easy for someone to overhear." I looked behind me. A reporter turned his eyes away from my screen. *Oops.* We'd have to use pencil and paper, not computers. Too bad.

I picked up my pencil and wrote, obscuring the page from any prying eyes, *I'll handle the bail, but it will take a while for them to process you out.*

I guess I should have kept the settlement money, she scribbled.

I agreed, but there was no point in bringing that up. I'd done very well as a defense attorney and had also pulled in a windfall when Jen and I handled a civil case against a deep-pocketed defendant. I'd put my share away for a rainy day. I'd handle Carly's bail through a bondsman I knew well. He'd put up the million, and it would cost us ten percent, or $100,000. Being accused of murder is expensive.

Conclusive Evidence

With a little luck we'd be able to get the charges dismissed at the preliminary hearing.

Chapter Seven

THE DAY BEFORE THE preliminary hearing, we gathered in my office. My conference table is meant for four, but we brought in an extra chair from Jen's office. Louella, Jen, Carly, Nicole, and I each had a coffee mug on the table. Jen's cup had her name and the words "World's Best Lawyer" written on it. Mine had my name and the same phrase, despite the logical impossibility. One Christmas, Nicole had given us those, and the next year I'd reciprocated with a "World's Best Law Student" mug, which she was too embarrassed to use at school.

The crackling fire made the gathering seem festive, and my mood was good. Nicole took on the job of translating, converting all of Jen's and Louella's words into ASL, and turning Carly's ASL into English. She was good at it.

Whenever Nicole or I had the floor, we spoke and signed simultaneously. I've never found it difficult to use the two languages at once, despite the differences in syntax.

I brought the meeting to order. "Don't get your hopes up, Carly, but we may be able to get the charges dismissed tomorrow. However, they may have some evidence they haven't revealed."

"Which is likely," Jen said.

I looked at her. "Because?"

"Because they'd have dropped this already if they didn't have something more. We know they have the supposed eyewitness and Carly's search history. They've got to know that you can knock those out of the water."

"We," I said.

"What?"

"We'll be doing this together. Don't forget."

"Right. Good thing, because being so close to this, I'm a little worried that you'll engage in wishful thinking. Why is it you don't think they have some secret weapon?"

"Crawford is desperate to get back at Carly. He'll do anything to embarrass her. If that means going ahead despite a lack of good evidence, he'll push for it."

"Push, yeah, but he's got to convince the DA. She's up for reelection soon, so she won't want to take any chances here."

I liked our DA, but she could be sneaky. In the past, Sibyl Finn had used underhanded strategies. I'd tried a case against her in which she closed with a PowerPoint presentation. The final slide showed the defendant, my client, in a booking photo with the word "GUILTY" stamped over him. In it, he wore orange prison garb. The state cannot force a defendant to wear prison clothing in court even if he isn't out on bail, because it undermines the presumption of innocence. I wasn't sure whether the photo had been Sibyl's error or someone else's, but I was able to convince the appeals court that it wasn't a harmless error. It's okay for advertisers to try to influence people subliminally, but not prosecutors. The verdict was reversed.

"What do you think, Louella?"

"Some people say he has something on Finn." Louella's smoker's baritone always surprised people who hadn't heard her speak, but we were used to it. "I disagree. She wouldn't pursue this case based only on the evidence they've shown us. There's got to be more."

"Hold on," Nicole said. "Wouldn't they have to give us their plans because of discovery?"

Many of the surprises that happen in television legal dramas can't happen in real life. That's because the law requires opposing sides in a legal dispute to share information. The prosecution must provide us with documents, reports, witness names, and so on, and we must do the same.

I answered, "That doesn't hold for the preliminary hearing. Besides, Sibyl tends to drag her feet on discovery. You don't have to provide materials the second you find out about them."

Jen pushed some of her thick hair behind an ear. "So we agree they probably have something else in their bag of tricks." She looked at me then shifted her eyes toward Carly and back again.

I got the message. "Carly, if there's anything you know of that could bite us, now's the time. If you want to talk with me privately, we can do that."

The ASL sign for "no" consists of two fingers being brought down on the thumb, like the beak of a bird closing. She made the sign once. Her expression added the exclamation mark. "No!"

"Okay, if they have something new, we'll deal with it. Louella, what do you have for us?"

Louella described her interview of the crabber, mentioning the collection of the tissue evidence from the boat hook. "And the police must have done their homework, because they knew that Angelo had a tattoo."

Carly sat up straight. "Tattoo?"

"On the back of his neck," Louella said.

"But Angelo doesn't have a tattoo."

That stopped us. The smell of the fire was getting a little intense. I went over and pushed the embers toward the back of the firebox.

"So it wasn't Angelo's body," Nicole said.

Jen tapped her fingernails on the table. "But the police think it was, right, Louella? Isn't that what your contact said?"

Louella took a cigarette out of her purse then put it back. "I'm guessing the tattoo is recent. When's the last time you saw him, Carly?"

"We separated before Christmas, last year. I've seen him around town since then, but I might not have noticed a tattoo. On the back of his neck?"

"Apparently."

"I could have missed it."

Louella nodded. "It sounds like it's new, then. The crabber said the colors looked fresh. Did he have any other tattoos?"

Carly signed, "No. He always thought they were stupid. Said that people didn't consider they'd have them for the rest of their lives."

"Do you think he could have changed his mind?" I asked.

She thought awhile then shrugged. "It's possible. Don't they have to have the body?" She fingerspelled "*habeas corpus.*"

"That the body must be found is a common misconception," Jen said. "You're actually thinking of *corpus delicti*, a term which means that the courts must prove a crime has been committed. '*Corpus*' is Latin for 'body,' but it doesn't refer to the body of the victim. It refers to the body of the *crime*. It's the principle that it must be proven a crime has been committed before someone can be prosecuted for it. But circumstantial evidence can be enough. In 1959, the case of People v. Leonard Ewing Scott cemented the idea that circumstantial evidence, if sufficient to exclude every other reasonable hypothesis, may prove the death of a missing person, the occurrence of a homicide, and the guilt of the accused."

Most would have had a *Well, excuse me!* look on their face. Carly wasn't like that. She recognized Jen as a fellow straightforward speaker. Many say that people in the deaf community are blunter than hearing people. It's been my experience, but I've been reluctant to admit it since it seems prejudiced.

I smiled. "Is that an exact quote, Jen?"

She replied, "Close enough."

I sipped some coffee, as if to punctuate the discussion. "Okay, so they have a much higher bar to clear without a body, but not insurmountable. Maybe we can attack the sighting, show reasonable doubt that it was Angelo. Maybe there wasn't enough tissue on the boat hook for a DNA analysis."

"What about the search history?" Nicole asked. "We can show an innocent explanation for that. Maybe we could knock down that idea, and they'd drop the charges."

"That's one option, sweetheart, and we might do that. But if it doesn't blow their case out of the water, bringing it up will just reveal our strategy. Better to let them use something as a leg for their case then kick it out from under them. It's a judgment call, and if their evidence seems weak tomorrow, we'll bring it up."

Louella said, "I want more leads on who else might have wanted Angelo dead. Carly?"

"We've been separated for a year," Carly said, "but even when we were married, he kept his shady business dealings a secret."

I made a note on my pad. "Can you give Louella a list of shady people or businesses he dealt with?"

She nodded. "What will happen tomorrow?"

"We don't know."

Carly slapped the table, making the coffee cups jump. "I'm not an idiot, bro. I mean what will be the procedure?"

"Sorry. In the preliminary hearing, the prosecution will attempt to show they have evidence that a crime was committed and that you committed it. If they can do that to the judge's satisfaction, you will be held to answer. That means there will be a trial. It may not seem fair, but the prosecution can put on witnesses, and we cannot. I can cross-examine them, however. Clear?"

"Yes."

"And I know you're good at this, but I'll say it anyway. Keep your expression neutral. No outbursts."

Carly's look said, *Duh*.

I stepped into Courtroom 4 as soon as the bailiff unlocked the doors. I liked to arrive early, relax, and soak in the atmosphere. The high ceiling held acoustic tiles with inset lighting. Maple paneling extended halfway up the walls on the sides of the room and all the way up in the front. Grayish industrial carpeting covered the floor. Courtrooms were the government's churches, but Humboldt County had built these temples on a budget.

The judge's bench was built into the corner, shoulder high, with an attached clerk's station: a sidecar on the motorcycle of authority. The low hum from the fluorescents in the ceiling would be lost once the room filled. They expected a crowd even though this was just a preliminary hearing. The case had been on the front page of the *Times Standard*.

I had my laptop, legal pad, travel mug, and pen arranged as I liked. I'm not obsessive about it, but it's good to have a well-organized base of operations, like a favorite chair at home.

The doors opened, and I turned. Carly walked up the aisle beside the DA, Sibyl Finn, as though they were casual friends on their way to a business meeting. Finn had gone with a pin-striped outfit once more, this time black instead of blue. Carly's outfit won the unintended competition based on points for elegance: a gray gabardine top with matching slacks that emphasized her long legs.

Although Carly had seen Finn at the arraignment, I introduced the two women. After they shook hands, Carly signed, "I didn't kill my husband," and I translated.

My mind flashed to the scene in the movie remake of *The Fugitive*, where Harrison Ford says, "I didn't kill my wife," and Tommy Lee Jones replies, "I don't care." But Finn did care. Very much. *How will she reply?*

"I'm pleased to meet you, Ms. Romero." Finn kept a cordial smile on her face. She asked me to come over and talk to her and then sat down at the prosecution table.

I wasn't able to tell what Carly was thinking from her face. She could be almost as inscrutable as Jen, even to her brother. I got her settled then stepped over and sat next to Finn.

She put her hand on my forearm. "Garrett, the new evidence I'm going to present just came in yesterday morning. I would have given you a heads-up if I'd had time."

Looking into her blue eyes, I sensed deceit, but perhaps it was my imagination. I'd never decided whether she was tough but fair, or just tough. I leaned toward the latter.

"What is it?"

"We had to get it translated, and that took some time." Her black outfit emphasized her pale skin. She had only a hint of freckles on her neck. She was going to make me wait, and I could handle that.

I shrugged as if in no rush even though the curiosity —and some anxiety—was burning a hole in my brain. "Tell me, Finn, you use that Irish brogue at home or only in public?"

She said a sentence or two, and I didn't understand a bit of it. Her voice lilted up and down, with some words that sounded like "quare," "fierce," and "yoke."

"Right." I put on my own version of her accent. "Sure'n ya should be talkin' like that all the time. Throw in a wee bit o' dancing, aye?"

She dropped her jaw and jerked her head back. "I sound like that? Like a Pakistani?"

I couldn't help but laugh, just as I couldn't help but like Finn. She has a way about her. Unlike Billy Joel, I did know what it was: a sense of calm confidence that impressed juries and judges.

Our banter was interrupted when the bailiff commanded us to "all rise," and Judge Irene Stevens swept into the court. "Swept" was a gross exaggeration, since she suffered from osteoporosis. When she walked, she resembled a lowercase "r" with a cane. I wasn't the only one who held his breath when she climbed the steps to the bench, breathing a sigh of relief when she didn't tumble out of view.

Stormy Stevens looked like a rich dowager from some Gilded Age English estate. Her long face was topped with yellow-white hair, and her inverted-V eyebrows looked as if someone had painted them on and way too high on her forehead. We were lucky to get her. Since the brain is a bone-free zone, her osteoporosis didn't affect her intellect. She was impartial and trustworthy, but cross her, and she lived up to her nickname. I'd once engaged in some courtroom theatrics that barely crossed the line, and the dressing down I received so diminished me in the eyes of the jurors that I only eked out a victory that should have been a slam dunk.

I went back to the defense table and sat between Carly and Jen.

Jen whispered in my ear, "The new evidence is a video, apparently."

The court clerk took care of the housekeeping, announcing the case number and so on.

Judge Stevens cleared her throat. "All right. Would counsel state their appearances for the record?"

"Good morning, Your Honor, Sibyl Finn for the People."

"Garrett Goodlove and Jen Shek for the defendant."

"Good morning," Stevens said. "Do you understand, Ms. Romero, that we are not here today to determine guilt or innocence, we are here only to determine whether this case should proceed to trial?"

Carly replied, "I do."

I'd explained that to her, and I'd made her understand that the level of proof was much lower than it would be if we went to trial. That is, the prosecution did not need to prove anything beyond a reasonable doubt. They just needed to show that there was a reasonable suspicion that a crime had been committed by Carly.

The ASL translator was the same one who'd been at the arraignment.

Judge Stevens turned to the prosecution table. "All right. Ms. Finn, are you prepared to call your first witness?"

"I am, Your Honor. The People call Mr. Zeke Kapkowski."

Most surfers here on the North Coast were older men with gray hair and yellowed longboards. Like me. Zeke looked more like a Southern California transplant. He had a bushy beard and scraggly hair that fell to his shoulders, as if he surfed so much he didn't have time for barbers. Or shaving. He wore a Hawaiian shirt with the top buttons undone and a surfboard pendant on a leather string around his neck. If he used the word "gnarly" or "stoked," I'd ask for a mistrial.

After the required preliminary questions, Finn asked, "Can you tell me what you saw while you were surfing on December third?"

"I saw someone fall off the cliff north of Camel Rock. That simple." Surprise. The board-head had a strong British accent.

"Tepona Point is about a thousand feet north of where you were surfing, does that sound right?"

"Yeah. Around three hundred meters."

"Yes. How did you happen to notice when he fell?"

"Just lucky, I guess. I heard a loud horn, maybe a car horn. It sounded like it came from that direction, but I didn't see anything. I went back to watching the waves, they were awesome that day, and then I guess I just happened to look that way again, and there's someone falling off the cliff. 'Tumbling' would be the word."

"Did it look like he jumped, fell, or was pushed?"

"He didn't jump, that's all that I can say, you know?"

"Why do you say that?"

"Well, I got the feeling that he bounced off part of the cliff as he fell. It wasn't like a swan dive or anything. It was messy. He was spinning in the air."

"What did you do then?"

"I would have paddled over to see if I could save the guy, but there are too many rocks between him and where I was. Big waves, too. Really gnarly."

Oof!

"Then what did you do?"

"I paddled in, ran up the path to the car, and called the police."

Finn said, "No further questions" and sat.

I went to the lectern. "Mr. Kapkowski, is the point you saw him fall from, straight down?"

"What do you mean?"

"I'm sorry, I mean, is it a straight shot down from the edge of the cliff to the water?" It wasn't. I'd checked it out from many angles.

"No, some of the rocks stick out."

"Did it seem that if someone took a running jump from the cliff, he could hit the water without hitting any rocks along the way?"

"Sure. I could do that. Sounds like fun, you know?"

"What if the jumper weren't so enthusiastic? Say, he was depressed or something? In that case—"

Finn stood. "Objection, Your Honor. Mr. Kapkowski isn't a psychologist."

"I'll allow it."

"In that case," I continued, "with someone who was depressed, who didn't feel like springing out from the edge of the cliff like an Olympic diver, would that person maybe hit the outcroppings along the way?"

"Yeah, sure."

"Or let's say the man just stood at the edge and let himself fall, would he hit the outcroppings? Could that be what you saw?"

"Yeah, maybe, but I had the feeling this guy didn't want to fall into the ocean."

"How do you figure that?"

Kapkowski chewed his lip. "Well, I can't really say. It's just a feeling, I guess."

"A feeling you got from a third of a kilometer away."

"Yeah, that's right."

"No further questions." Had I gotten the judge to consider that whoever dropped off that cliff may have been committing suicide? Hard to say. Stevens was smart; she'd probably already considered that. I wasn't worried that I'd tipped my hand with my questions, since it was an obvious defense: *My client didn't do it. Angelo committed suicide.*

"The People call Mr. Wenzel Rozetti, Your Honor."

Finn had established that someone fell into the ocean. Next, she needed to demonstrate that that person was Angelo Romero, and that he was dead.

Finn brought the crabber to the stand and ran him through his description of seeing but not retrieving Angelo's body, returning to port, and handing over the boat hook to Detective Crawford. It matched what Louella had described to me.

Finn returned to her chair.

When I didn't get up right away, Stevens cleared her throat. "Mr. Goodlove?"

"Excuse me a second, Your Honor." I whispered to Jen, "What do you think?"

She put her mouth up to my ear, shielding it with a hand. "Pass. Nothing to be gained. Angelo's dead. We knew that."

"Agreed." I turned to the judge. "No questions, Your Honor."

"The People call Detective Damon Crawford."

"Just a moment." Stevens leaned forward. "How many more witnesses are you going to call?"

I looked at Crawford, who had just stood up. When we locked eyes, he brought up his hand and shot me with a finger pistol.

Finn looked at her notes. "Only five more, Your Honor."

"Uh, no. That's too many. Why so many?"

"Detective Crawford lays the foundation for some evidence regarding Mr. Rozetti's boat hook, and I have a witness who will describe the collection of hair from Angelo Romero's apartment."

"I think we can save that for the trial, if there is one."

Finn nodded. "In that case, I will call Dr. Olga Magroski."

Ah, the DNA expert I'd consulted concerning the sperm "donation" case. She had the same big smile and flyaway blonde hair, but instead of a lab coat, she wore a wrap dress with flowers on a black background.

Finn began running through her qualifications. I stipulated that she had the necessary expertise, and we got down to the meat of the matter.

"Dr. Magroski," Finn said, "did you analyze the boat hook Mr. Rozetti used to try to retrieve the body he discovered in the ocean?"

"I did."

"And can you tell us what you found?"

"Sure. There were some cheek cells—like those you'd get by scraping the inside of your mouth with a swab—on the boat hook as well as some other organic material. There was degradation of the material, as you'd expect if the body had been in the ocean."

"Thank you. Did you extract the DNA and compare it with DNA from the hair samples we'd provided you?"

"Yes. And they matched."

"The DNA analysis showed that the tissue on the boat hook and the hair came from the same individual?"

"With an extremely high probability, yes."

"No further questions."

It would have helped if the DNA didn't match. No point in a cross-examination. I looked at Jen to confirm, and she shook her head.

"No questions, Your Honor."

"Without objection, we will recess for lunch." Stevens banged her gavel when neither Finn nor I opposed the break.

Things didn't look good for getting the charges dismissed. My cautious optimism had been wishful thinking. Finn had established that someone had fallen off the cliff. Given that Angelo's car was abandoned in the parking lot and his DNA was on the boat hook, it followed that Angelo was dead.

Finn's next task wouldn't be as easy. She had to show a reasonable suspicion that Carly had pushed him to his death.

Chapter Eight

CARLY, JEN, AND I had lunch at The Hangar Cafe at Murray Field. The county-owned public airport catered mostly to private planes, and the greasy spoon served the best $100 hamburgers in the area. They didn't cost us $100, that term was some aviation humor referring to pilots who wanted an excuse to fly. They'd get in their small plane, fly for a few hours, have lunch, and fly back. The cost of those burgers was $100. Probably a lot more.

The only other diners were a pilot and his wife, who were unlikely to know ASL. I explained our situation to Carly. She bit her lip, something she used to do as a teenager when she was stressed. I was seeing the first cracks in her stoicism. She had circles under her eyes.

"I would die in prison," she said. "I wouldn't be able to communicate. It would be like solitary confinement."

"Hey. It's *way* too early to panic, sis. Our hands are tied now, but we'll be able to punch back if it goes to trial."

Jen turned her face to Carly. "Garrett is very good at that."

Carly nodded. She'd speech-read. I didn't tell her that the toughest part might be the months leading up to that trial. The suspense.

We finished our burgers and went back to court.

When the judge was ready, Finn rose. "The People call Ms. Yvette Dowzer."

Ms. Dowzer was a fit and somewhat trim senior citizen with long white hair.

After some preliminaries, Finn asked, "Ms. Dowzer, can you tell us what you saw on the morning of December third?"

"I had just parked my car down the street a bit. I was going to walk along Scenic Drive. I know it was a little after ten. I'd just listened to part of the news. KHSU. I saw the woman when I was at the start of the trail."

"Was this the short trail to Tepona Point?"

"Well, I didn't know that then, the name of the place where I was. But after I saw the news that night about what happened, about the man who was pushed off—"

"Move to strike, Your Honor."

"Sustained." Judge Stevens turned to the witness. "Please testify only about what you observed, Ms. Dowzer."

"Okay. Sorry. I heard about what happened, and they talked about Tepona Point on the news. I looked it up on Google, on the maps. I saw that that was where I was. Tepona Point. I like to go out there and look at the view. The waves were very big."

"And what happened then?"

"Right. Well, there are a few steps up from the parking lot. There's the trail along that ridge there that goes out to the point. I had just gone up the steps, when a woman came rushing up the trail. She had on a green sweatshirt. It was a hoodie. It had the name of Bizet University. The deaf school here, you know. She was in a hurry. She had her head down."

"Were you able to see her face?"

"Only for a second."

"Is that woman here in the courtroom today?"

"Well, I'm pretty sure, yes. Yes, she is. Can I point?"

"You may." Finn stood aside to give the woman a clear view of Carly.

Ms. Dowzer pointed to my sister.

"Let the record show that the witness pointed to the defendant."

Carly wrote on my pad. *Not me!* She underlined it hard enough to rip the paper.

Finn continued, "Ms. Dowzer, was the woman scared?"

"Objection. Your Honor, the witness apparently only got a quick glance at the woman's face. Even if Ms. Dowzer were an expert at interpreting facial expressions—"

"Your Honor, I think most people are able to tell when someone is—"

"Sustained. Please rephrase the question."

"Yes, Your Honor. Ms. Dowzer, can you tell us anything more about what you saw?"

Of course, the witness then knew exactly what Finn was asking, but her response was a gift to us. "Well, I do admit that I only got a very quick look at her face. Just a flash, you know. I guess I kinda felt that the woman was scared because she was rushing, as I said. I may have said that to the policeman, Mr. Crawford, when he asked, but now, you know, I'm not really sure."

Finn didn't want to leave it on that note. "But you are sure the woman you saw is now sitting there at the defense table?"

"Objection. Asked and answered." I put a bored tone in my voice, like, *Oh, gee, this is so lame.* I had no jury to play to, but habits are hard to break.

"Sustained."

Finn sat down. I stood and stepped to the lectern. "Thank you, Ms. Dowzer, for contacting the police about this. They rely on helpful citizens like you, and many people would have decided to not get involved."

She smiled self-consciously.

"Did you contact the police when you saw this woman?"

"No, no. Of course not. It was only when I saw the story on the local news. I realized I was at the exact place, Tepona Point. I was there when the man—when the thing happened. I told my husband the next morning. He said, 'You know, Yvette, maybe you should call the police. Maybe that woman was involved somehow.' So that's what I did. I called the sheriff's office."

"And what happened then?"

"Well, they said they'd send a police officer to my house. I told them where it was. Maybe they already knew. Because of the telephone system, you know. Caller ID."

"Then what happened?"

"Well, Detective Crawford drove up and came into the house. I told him my story. He took out a photograph and asked me, 'Is this the woman?' I said yes."

"How sure were you at that point, when he first showed you the photo?"

She looked toward the ceiling as if the answer were written there. "Well, maybe not so sure then. But I've played it over. In my head. I realized that it was her."

"Did he just show you the one photo?"

"Well, then he did, yeah. Later, when I went to the police station, they showed me what he called a six-pack because it was six photographs of women. And I picked out the same woman as before. The same one as is sitting here."

"No further questions, Your Honor."

Next up was Ms. Rice, a woman with skin that looked somehow artificial—like a realistic Japanese robot I once saw on TV. She was an RPPD technician who dealt with electronic evidence. As expected, Finn led her through Carly's search history, showing that she'd sought information on how to kill someone. "How to murder someone and not get caught" was one of the more dramatic examples, sending a wave of murmurs through the spectators. I saw a reporter friend of mine rush out of the courtroom.

When Finn was done, I said, "No questions, Your—"

Carly hit my arm. Hard.

"Just a moment, Your Honor."

Carly wrote, *Tell them!!!* on my pad.

Trust me, I wrote back. I didn't have time to explain.

Jen put her finger on my words and nodded at Carly.

Carly never liked being ganged up on. She crossed her arms, sat back, and fluttered her lips, not understanding how loud it was. Also not understanding that it could be interpreted as frustration that she'd been "found out." I clenched my jaw.

I stood, said, "I have no questions for this witness," and sat.

I was beginning to hope that the rumors Jen had heard about a video were unfounded. That hope was dashed when the plasma screens on both sides of the courtroom flickered on.

Finn stood with the flare of a magician about to reveal her ultimate trick. "May it please the Court, I will now play a video recording that is germane to this case. In the interest of saving time, I will not present the foundation for this evidence, based on your comments earlier. A Ms. Suzy Pickerel recently contacted the police department. She had seen a sign-language conversation between a woman she recognized as the defendant and someone else. This took place in the Starbucks inside the Target store on Fourth Street. Pickerel was learning ASL and knew enough to understand what was being said. When she heard about Mr. Romero's death, she reported the conversation to the police, and we obtained the security camera footage from the coffee shop. Thus, we were able to view the conversation for ourselves."

Jen was up in a flash. "Your Honor, surely the prosecution knows that eavesdropping is a crime in California."

"Only when it's recorded, Your Honor," Finn said.

Jen pointed at the video screens, which held a static image of the RPPD logo. "As it was in this case."

"But not by Ms. Pickerel. If she'd recorded the conversation, we'd agree that it was both illegal and inadmissible. That's not what we have here. The footage was recorded by an uninterested party in a public place."

I stood. "Your Honor, this is a complete surprise to us. May I have a few minutes to confer with my client?"

"Go ahead," she replied.

I scrawled, *Do you know what this is about?* on my pad.

She wrote, *Maybe. I talked with Bridget. Mad at Angelo.*

What did you say?

Don't remember.

Aargh. I couldn't show my anger, since I felt everyone's eyes on me. Jen and I whispered together for a bit. I counted to ten, then said, "Thank you for that, Your Honor. We are ready now and object to this testimony being brought in."

Judge Stevens turned her attention to the prosecutor. "Do you have any relevant case law, Ms. Finn?"

"I do. In Washington State, a man called his cell phone from his landline, attempting to find it. The cell phone was somewhere in the room. He didn't locate it but inadvertently left the line open, and the phone's voicemail was activated. Thus, it recorded the altercation with his wife in which he beat her extensively and shouted, 'I am going to kill you.'"

Jen said, "Your Honor—"

Stevens held up her hand like a traffic cop, her eyes on Finn. "Anything else?"

"Yes. In Wyoming, through a series of mishaps, a woman's Alexa device thought it heard the word, 'Alexa.' It then recorded the woman's conversation. When it thought the woman said, 'Send message,' the device asked, 'To whom?' It thought it heard the name of one of the woman's contacts, thought the woman confirmed the send, and sent an MP3 of the conversation. Improbable as it may seem, that really happened, and the recording was used as evidence that the woman had received and used insider trading information."

Jen was still standing. "Your Honor, California is much more stringent than Wyoming when it comes to privacy laws. I'm sure we can show that this recording is inadmissible."

Judge Stevens closed her eyes, her fingers on her lips, and her head rocking forward and back. Finally, she returned from her fugue. "I'm going to allow it for the preliminary hearing."

I stood and took a breath, wanting to ensure that I didn't sound whiny. "Your Honor, can we at least clear the courtroom? This could taint the jury pool."

"Do you even know what this conversation is about, counselor?"

"I do not. This is the first I'm hearing about it. All I know is that it may be a private conversation my client had with her best friend."

"In a public place," Finn said, coming close to addressing me rather than the judge.

Jen kept her voice calm. "People have private conversations in public places all the time with the objectively reasonable expectation that electronic devices will not be used to record them. The intent of California's privacy law matches this situation clearly. Security cameras don't have microphones, but because of the special circumstances in this situation they were able to record the conversation that our client had."

"We will view the video in my chambers." Stevens rapped her gavel.

Back we went to the judge's chambers—Stevens, Jen, Finn, and me. The room was surprisingly homey, filled with decades of mementos and photographs. It also had the old-person smell that reminded me of a nursing home.

Finn slid the DVD into the judge's player. "This is a conversation between Ms. Romero and a woman we've identified as Ms. Bridget Dundon."

Bridget had been Carly's best friend for as long as I could remember. She lost her hearing in infancy due to an illness.

Finn continued, "We had our translator add subtitles to the video. This is of course her interpretation. As you'll see, the camera was side on to the—"

"Let's watch it now, Ms. Finn," Stevens said.

The video, in color, came up in a freeze-frame, displaying the camera number, the date, and the time at the bottom left. Carly and Bridget sat in a booth toward the back of the room. They had evidently begun the conversation earlier—perhaps when getting their coffee —so we missed the start.

Finn pressed Play.

Dundon: But what do you care? You're separated.

Romero: It was going on for a long time. We were mourning the death of Patricia, and he was out screwing like a coked-up rabbit. He should have been home for me. I can't forgive him.

Dundon: What did she say?

Romero: She'd seen Angelo with another woman. From a distance. They were kissing in a romantic way. She thought it was me, but when she got closer, she saw it was someone else. She didn't want to break my heart. She saw them again after we'd separated. She decided she should tell me.

Dundon: But you shouldn't have cared.

Romero: It's the principle of the thing. I'm going to kill him … I'm going to push him off a fucking cliff.

When she said, "I'm going to kill him," I gave a little laugh. *Is that all they've got?* People say things like that all the time without meaning it. Without breaking a sweat I could get the jury to understand that it was just a figure of speech. But when she said, "I'm going to push him off a fucking cliff," my heart felt as if it had been flash frozen.

I saw two possibilities. The first was plain bad luck. He just happened to die in a way that matched her prophecy. But what a monumental coincidence. When it came to a jury, would it be a fluke that was beyond belief? The second possibility was that Carly did it. If that recording could shake my confidence in her, a perfect stranger would see it as a smoking gun. The only way it could have been worse would be if she'd said, "I'm going to push him off Tepona Point on December third at ten thirteen a.m."

I've heard it many times before: *Oh, so-and-so could never kill someone. It's just not in him.* But I'd learned that anyone can commit murder under the right circumstances. Worse, Carly never struck me as someone who wouldn't hurt a fly. She was tough and strong, and if she believed something was right, she'd do it. The only other person in our family who was like that was Toby, but to a lesser degree.

Jen and I restated our objection on the basis of privacy laws, and the judge invited me to submit a motion to suppress it. Stevens's body language spoke loud and clear: She would rule in my favor.

We reconvened in court. Judge Stevens ruled that Carly would be held to answer. There would be a trial. We scheduled jury selection for April 5.

When Nicole was a teenager, before Raquel died, she had a poster in her room with a photo of two screaming parents. The overlying text read, "Adolescence: a time when parents are irrational." Just as teenagers see their parents as the ones acting differently, a depressed person may not recognize that his own feelings are altering his perception of others. Of reality. For example, when I was depressed, I was convinced it was the kids who started fights with me, or who were intentionally antagonizing me. I remember yelling at Toby because he had trouble operating our new DVR even though I also found the interface confusing. It wasn't until my return to sanity that the true dynamic revealed itself.

That understanding should have made me avoid Crawford after the depressing ruling. I wasn't in my right mind.

The hallway on the second floor of the courthouse is a disheartening place no matter what mood you're in.

The tile floor reflected the harsh lighting and echoed the hopeless conversations of the accused. A row of stained plywood benches extended down the center of the hall. Despite the signs prohibiting it, Crawford sat on the back of a bench, his feet where his butt belonged. Like a vulture waiting for dead meat, he focused his eyes on me as I exited the courtroom. I resolved to ignore him, but it wasn't to be.

He imitated the *dun dun duuun* musical phrase that often accompanied a dramatic turn of events in 1940s movies, then said, "Judgment day is coming."

I stopped and tried to count to ten, but I only got to three. "I agree."

"You agree?"

"Yeah. Judgment day is coming for you. This case never would have come this far if not for your personal vendetta against my sister. Even with one arm tied behind my back I'll be able to show that—"

Someone grabbed my elbow, almost pulling my arm from its socket.

It was Jen. My partner was small but strong. She dragged me down the hall toward the stairwell. "You know better than that, boss."

I snapped at her. "What? I can't talk with the detective on the case?"

We turned into the stairwell, and she pushed me against the wall. "You taught me: You set your own schedule for discussions. You think, you plan, you prepare, and you sure as hell don't let someone goad you into saying something stupid." She was right.

I took a breath then laughed.

She narrowed her eyes. "What?"

"When you pushed me against the wall, I thought maybe you were going to kiss me again." We both looked up, as if someone might have taped a sprig of mistletoe onto the flaking cement of the ceiling.

"In your dreams." She took my arm, and we started down the marijuana-scented stairs.

"So, what do you think?"

"I think we have our work cut out for us."

We came out on the ground floor and pushed through the exit doors. I kept my voice low. "You know what I mean. Do you think Carly did it?"

"What do we always tell our clients?"

I said it with a singsong in my voice. "Doesn't matter what I think, it's what the jury thinks. But we both know that's just a bullshit way of deflecting the question. It distracts the client by making him picture the jury giving a verdict. That makes him forget that it would actually help if his lawyer believed him to be innocent. It doesn't give him a chance to think, *If my own lawyer doesn't believe me, what chance do I have with a jury?*"

"You're losing your objectivity here, boss. I'm not sure you can function well as a lawyer if you're acting like a loving brother. Emotion isn't your friend here."

"That's why I have you."

"Damn right."

We reached my car. Before I unlocked it, I looked over the roof at my partner. "Really, Jen, do you think my sister could have tossed her husband into the ocean?"

"Physically?"

"Emotionally."

She gave me her patented neutral look. "Doesn't matter what I think." *Did she practice that in the mirror?*

Chapter Nine

CARLY LEANED BACK ON my office couch, and I perched on the edge of an overstuffed leather chair from the early 1900s. She and I were alone in the office. As always, I had a fire going. I found the crackling soothing, and I hoped the heat could warm the cold heart of my twin sister. The shock that she would soon be on trial for murder was only a few hours old.

Despite the grim circumstances, my heart had been warmed by the rekindling of my relationship with her. *Should I feel guilty that I'm grateful for the events that brought us back together?* A chance encounter in the checkout lane of the grocery store might have been better than a murder indictment, but fate works in mysterious ways.

"It's too early to worry, sis."

"You'll let me know when it's time?" Her reply was half humor, half admonishment. Carly wasn't a big fan of platitudes.

I took a moment to plan our conversation. The crackling fire did its magic but also triggered my frustration over Carly's disability. She was adamant that she was happy being deaf. In her view, deaf people aren't disabled, they just have a different way of communicating—a different language! Very true as far as language was concerned, but there was a lot more to hearing. Even sitting there in my office, the tapestry of sounds added a richness to my life: the murmurs from Jen's office as she consulted with a new client, the occasional tone of the foghorn in the channel, the scratching noises that told me the building was once again infested with mice, even the annoying bass from the sound system of a passing car. When I was a kid, I'd foolishly tried to prove to Carly that she didn't know what she was missing.

I've always had a wicked ringing in my ears—something called "tinnitus"—and I sometimes wished it would go away, just for a few minutes. But that yearning was stupid. If I could experience a few minutes of blessed relief, the tinnitus would bother me even more for the rest of my life. In the same way, why make Carly appreciate something she could never have? Ignorance is bliss. 'Tis folly to be wise.

Anyone could be happy, even those with a more severe disability than deafness. *Was Carly happy?*

She kicked me in the shin.

"*Ow!*"

"Did you go to Bermuda in your mind?"

We both laughed. That was an expression we used to use when referring to daydreaming. Some things are funnier when expressed in sign, and Carly has impeccable timing. Maybe she *was* happy.

"Are you happy, Carly?"

She replied right away. "Happier than you."

Whoa! I was recovering, but maybe she had a point. Of course, it was *her* daughter who had died, but I'd lost a wife *and* a niece. No, that wasn't how happiness worked. It didn't have a scorecard.

On to business. "First, Carly, you are going to have to control yourself in court."

She cocked her head, looking like a puzzled puppy. "What the hell do you mean?"

I blew out my breath, causing my lips to flutter. I pointed to them and exaggerated the effect so much that it sounded like a horse to me.

She sat there.

"When I didn't cross-examine the woman who talked about your browser history and told you to trust me, that's what you did. It made a loud noise that everyone in the courtroom heard. I understand you were expressing your frustration that I wasn't doing what you wanted me to, but that's not how it would have been interpreted by others."

"Why didn't you tell them why I did those searches?"

"We'll come back to that. I want to explain how it might have been construed by others. Like this: The witness says, 'She searched for how to murder someone,' and you respond by saying, 'Oh, crap. They caught me.'"

"Oh. Who would think that?"

"Anyone," I said. "But more importantly, a juror might think that. It's the way people are. One little thing can tip them over into having a particular point of view, and it can be hard to switch them back. Maybe that one juror would hold sway with others in the deliberation room: 'Hey, did everyone notice how she reacted when they uncovered her search history?'"

"Okay, got it."

"I want you to be a statue out there. Don't make eye contact; look down at the pad in front of you."

"Okay, okay. But why didn't you tell them why I searched for those things?"

"It was a judgment call based on years of experience."

She fluttered her lips—*joking?*

"By then I was pretty sure we'd be going to trial. If so, not tipping my hand gives me a secret weapon. We know something they don't."

"But they will figure it out."

"Maybe, maybe not. Let's imagine for a second that they build their whole case around your searches. We can go in there and unravel all their work. But if they know ahead of time—"

"Okay, okay. I got it. No outbursts. Trust you."

"I couldn't have said it better."

She got up and went to the coffee maker, refilled her cup. When she came back, I pointed to the cup. "Aren't you going to have trouble sleeping?"

She put it on the side table. "You're the one with insomnia."

"What? How did you know about that? We weren't talking back then."

She shrugged. "I keep track of my baby brother."

My being born five minutes after her made me her baby brother. It was a running joke for us back when we were inseparable.

"That's nice to know, actually." I used a sign that wasn't part of ASL. Most people are aware that some twins develop their own private language. Carly and I had done the same, creating a sign language that only we understood. We'd had a sign that meant *"nice to know."*

She laughed. "I'd almost forgotten!"

I was reluctant to destroy the nostalgia and feelings that were building, but we had business to conduct. I said, "I'm very angry that you didn't tell me about that conversation with Bridget!" Carly hadn't seen the video, but I'd shown her the transcript.

She rocked her head like Stevie Wonder.

"What does that mean?"

"It was a private conversation. How was I to know it would be recorded?"

"This is serious! I can't defend you properly if you don't tell me everything. Let me be the judge of what's important."

"If you'd known ahead of time, would things be different?"

"Yes!" I signed "yes" twice to put an exclamation mark on it. "We could have researched the case law, presented a convincing argument, and perhaps the judge never would have seen the recording. Then maybe she wouldn't have held you to answer, and you would be free right now. This whole nightmare would be over."

That hit home more strongly than I intended. Tears welled in her eyes. Perhaps through our twin bond, I felt her pain. The terrible dagger to the heart of the words "if only." I sat beside her and took her hand. I hadn't seen her cry since that day in third grade when some boys at the park teased her and threw rocks. I got some pleasure out of beating the crap out of the ringleader, but all she got was the message: *You are different.* No wonder many deaf individuals end up with a prejudice against the hearing world.

After we sat that way for ten minutes, I moved back to my chair, facing her. "Why did you say you would throw Angelo off a cliff?"

"I said, 'push.'"

"Okay." Push was worse, of course, since it was more feasible. Angelo was a big guy. "Why that expression? So specific?"

"We lived so close to the cliffs over the ocean. On Scenic Drive. It seemed more real to say that. If I said I was going to throw him out of a helicopter, it wouldn't feel real, since I don't have one. I recall that I was going to say, 'I'm going to fucking strangle him,' but then a picture of me pushing him off Wedding Rock jumped into my head. So I said what I said."

I leaned forward and patted her on the knee. "It was just bad luck. We'll get through this, I'm not worried." *Was I lying?* "Now you need to tell me why you were so angry with Angelo, even though you've been separated for—what?"

"A year."

"Right."

She took her time organizing her thoughts. "Angelo was a bad person. A bad human being."

She didn't have to tell me that. Before they were married, Carly seemed to be the only person who didn't see it. Or maybe she didn't care.

"But he had a special attraction for me, like a spider attracting a fly," she said. "Everyone told me to stay away from him. Maybe that was the problem."

"You don't like being told what to do."

"Correct. Surprisingly, the marriage went well for many years. At first, he was gung ho about learning ASL. He lost his enthusiasm for that, but he was easy to speech-read, and we communicated well. When I was pregnant, I had this feeling that he was cheating on me. I couldn't believe it, though, and I ignored the signs."

"Is that why you separated?"

"Don't get ahead of me. No. That was after Patricia … died. Do I have to explain?"

I shook my head. A great tragedy can pull a marriage together or break it apart. For them, apparently, it was the latter.

She explained anyway. "I needed him after that, and he could have made things better. He could have … comforted me. We could have comforted each other. But he was distant. It was bad."

I'd wanted to comfort her, but she wouldn't let me close.

"Around Thanksgiving, I got an email," Carly said. "Wait, I'll show you. Give me the laptop."

On the MacBook—the clone of the one the police had —she brought up Gmail.

Dear Carly Romero:

You dont know me. I am loosing my hearing and I no you from the news etc. Im not good with english. It is not my first language. I wasn't going to tell this you but i herd that you are now divorcing from your husband and I think this information may be important for you.

I don't know if you know but your husband was having an affair. I saw him doing that in 2014, when you were having a baby. I was at a hotel in Fortuna and I was in the lobby and I thought I saw you and Angelo checking in. I was going to come and introduce myself. I thought it was you that he was with then I got closer and then I saw that she wasn't pregnant. So I stayed back.

Any way, they were kissing, and I saw them go to a room together.

I'm sorry if I'm not minding my own business. Maybe this will help you with the animony or something.

"I'm sorry, Carly. I had no idea."

"That opened my eyes. I discussed it with my friends. He was having this affair all along. Right up until …"

"I can understand how that makes you feel."

A blush spread up from her neck and onto her cheeks. "Can you? I don't think so. The whole time that Patricia was alive and then when she died. No wonder he wasn't there for me. How could he have possibly done that? You know what I wish?" Her jaw muscles stood out.

"What?"

"I wish he was still alive so I could kill him."

At least she didn't say "kill him *again*."

"Carly, you are not to say anything like that. Not to me, not to anyone."

"Are you saying I was wrong to have that conversation with Bridget?"

I thought about it. "No. A lot of people say they want to kill someone even though they don't really mean it." I would have added *"You didn't really mean it, did you?"* but I was pretty sure I wouldn't like the answer.

"I meant it." Carly always could read my mind.

"It was just bad luck that you said it the way you did and worse luck that the conversation was recorded. Now, there's something else we need to discuss. Finn called and offered a plea deal. It—"

Carly signed, "No."

"I have to present it to you. If you were to plead to second-degree murder, she would recommend a sentence of fifteen years."

"I would rather die than be in prison for fifteen years. You don't think I should take that plea, do you?"

I had hoped Carly would say she wasn't going to plead guilty to something she didn't do. In any case, it was too early to consider a plea like that.

"No." I shook my head. "I don't. We're going to try to exclude the recording of the conversation as well as the eyewitness testimony. Do *not* get your hopes up, but if we can do that, they might drop the charges."

It was Louella's first day on the job, and she was getting DialUSA's orientation tour, led by a Mr. Kim. He was tall and frightfully thin—*maybe he was from North Korea?*

—and his accent made it seem as if he weren't even speaking English.

She looked over the sea of call stations, whose dividers consisted of unpainted plywood. Four across and six deep. Twenty-four stations. She only saw a few who were old enough to have ever actually "dialed" a phone. A haze of smoke drifted near the buzzing lights. Since the building sat on tribal land, it was exempt from no-smoking laws, like many of the casinos.

"Is those computers broken?" *Am I overdoing it?* Louella was playing the part of a down-and-out old lady, living in her car, desperate for even the worst kind of job. Given Kim's accent, he probably couldn't hear the difference between ghetto Ebonics and Oxford English.

"No. Need more workers. Is lucky for you."

"And the company is doing good?"

"Yes. Very good." Kim spoke with a rapid staccato, like a machine gun.

Louella lit a cigarette and thought about her research. Call centers like this in the Philippines survived on the backs of low-wage employees. The slaves started at 13,000 pesos a month. Twenty-one cents an hour. So how could this company survive? It couldn't. Her working theory was that what she was seeing was just a front.

"Here your station." Kim stopped at a computer and headset in the last row. It couldn't be called a cubicle since it had plywood on only three sides. He booted up the computer. "Computer do all the work. Call people; wait for answer. When scrip come here, you read. Okay?"

"Script," she said without thinking, emphasizing the T.

"Yes, scrip. Understand? Lunch at twelve. Go home at six. Come to me if have questions." He pointed to a corner of the room with a real desk.

So much for worker training. More proof that their real business lay elsewhere. Louella got comfortable and started working. Perhaps it was her smoker's baritone that did the trick, but by midafternoon, she'd closed the sale of two whole life insurance policies.

When the poor schmuck on the other end of the line asked a question, the computer interpreted it and displayed a response for Louella to read. *Won't be long before they don't need humans at all.* There were only a few times when the computer's suggested reply was inappropriate, and for those, Louella composed her own answer. *This is why I earn the big bucks.*

She did only minor snooping on that first day, talking with coworkers in the bathroom—no help there—checking for locked doors, watching for activity that didn't fit.

At the end of the second day, she hid in a closet when it was quitting time. No one worked late. She spent an hour in the closet until her bladder demanded a trip to the bathroom. *Am I getting too old for this?* She cracked the door and listened. No sign of a night watchman yet.

After answering the call of nature, she headed to the locked door that held the most promise. She pulled the Kronos Electropik from her purse. It resembled an electric toothbrush with a thin blade in place of a brush head. It actually functioned a lot like a toothbrush, but instead of flushing plaque out from between your teeth, it flushed a lock's pins out of the keyway. To turn a lock, all of the pins need to line up. The Electropik bounces the pins up and down while the tension tool, nothing more than a bent piece of metal, gently urges the cylinder to turn. On a cheap lock, like the one in front of Louella, it takes only seconds until the pins line up.

Sure enough, ten seconds of buzzing did the trick, and she was in. She closed the door, locked it, and switched on the light.

The size of a double garage, the place had none of the third-world unpainted plywood feel of the main room. High-tech office chairs sat at several workstations with keyboards and curved computer screens. The highlight, however, was the electronics equipment stacked on four racks against one wall.

Louella started snapping photos and recording video as she scanned her phone down each rack, getting closeups of the unfamiliar electronics. Someone would know what this stuff did. She also got footage of the manuals on the shelves.

She recognized a Mac Mini below one of the monitors and was tempted to slip it into her purse. No. This was a stealth operation and might not even be relevant to Romero's death. All she had was the coincidence of Rozetti and Romero working for the same small company, the crabber's contention that he didn't know Romero, and the strangeness of the company. There was something funky going on, but it could be unrelated to Angelo.

She walked to the door, her work done. *No more telemarketing for me.* She froze. *Voices. Plural!* Unlikely they'd have two night watchmen. Whoever it was might come into the room. *Crap.*

If she could get out of the room before they arrived, she could say she fell asleep or something. That wouldn't work. She could point her gun at them—not ideal. She looked around the room. *No closets but—*

The voices came closer, arguing.

She switched off the light and shook her phone to activate the flashlight. The electronics racks were far enough from the wall to allow rear access to the wiring. She slid in sideways then squatted slightly, her back against the wall and her arthritic knees pushed into the recess of one of the racks.

The door slammed open and the lights flashed on.

"—because we're losing a fucking ten thousand dollars a day, that's why." The man's voice was gruff with a New York City accent.

"On average."

"What?"

The other man's voice suggested a smaller person, no detectable accent. "You're losing ten thousand a day on average. Some days—"

"Hey! You know what? It's none of your fucking business. They told me it's got to be fixed tonight, and that's what you're going to do. I'll show you the problem."

They said nothing as switches clicked, fans began whirring, and LEDs flashed on the equipment. Louella looked down. Her foot lay on a power cable to a heavy-duty power strip, and the plug had pulled halfway out of the socket. She inched her arm down to push it in but couldn't reach. Already her right knee was sending flashes of pain up her body. She pictured the equipment snapping off and the bad guys investigating—finding an elderly black woman hunched over between the racks and the wall. *Surprise!*

The two men said nothing, but clicks from a keyboard reached her ears.

A new voice rang out. "I am totally stuck here, and I'm out of money. I know I was stupid, but if you wire the money, I can pay you back." This voice sounded like someone imitating a robot. The words were totally monotonic. No intonation up or down.

"There. See?" New York said. "That's gonna work about as good as Godzilla in a whorehouse."

"Well, shit. You could have told me that over the phone."

A slap sounded.

"Hey, what'd you do that for?"

"'Cause you don't fuckin' talk to me like that. Can you fix it or not?"

"Some dipshit didn't patch in the modulator. Like this."

A sharp *snap* sounded and a new fan whirred into life. Heat was already flowing back over Louella's body, and sweat tickled its way down her sides.

"Now listen," the smaller man said.

"I am totally stuck here, and I'm out of money. I know I was stupid, but if you wire the money, I can pay you back." That time, the voice was perfect. After the fix, the woman's voice sounded natural, filled with fear and frustration.

Little Man said, "See? Next time, you give me a call and tell me what's wrong. I had to drive up here all the way from Ferndale. There was no need for me to come here."

"We don't talk about this stuff over the fucking phone."

"Sheesh. When you call my phone, no one can listen in. Trust me." Someone started powering down the equipment. "Besides, you don't need to give away the whole store. For this, if you'd just said, 'The voices are monotonic,' I could have told you which switch to throw. Yeah, maybe you don't know the word 'monotonic' but—ow! Hey look, you need me a lot more than I need you."

The lights switched off and the door closed. The angry voices receded.

"Aaah!" Louella straightened up. She switched on her flashlight. The power cord had fallen out of the socket. She sidled out from behind the racks then got on her knees, reached in, and plugged the cord back into the wall.

Louella left the room and the building, locking the doors behind her.

Chapter Ten

MID-JANUARY, JEN AND I were talking strategy when someone entered the empty reception area. Nicole had gone back to law school, and I hadn't yet hired someone to take her place.

A voice reached us. "Hello?"

I stepped out of my office to find none other than Isabel Sheridan standing there. She was the California state senator for our district and perhaps the most popular politician on the West Coast.

She took off her coat and draped it over her arm. "You're Garrett Goodlove."

"I am." I shook her hand. "Let me take your coat."

"I've seen you on the news, and I've come to you because I have a problem."

On the few occasions I've encountered women who are famous for their beauty, seeing them in person far outstripped the TV or silver screen experience. I've never understood that.

Ms. Sheridan had a perpetual tan that I'm sure came from genetics rather than sun exposure, concave cheeks that had nothing to do with food deprivation, and a bearing that suggested royalty. Her hair was the color of almonds, short, with a wave that came low over one eye and swept back toward her ear. Her nose was exceptionally long and narrow, adding to her aristocratic aura.

I brought her into my office and introduced her to Jen. I put another log on the fire and asked her how we might help.

"Are you taking on any new clients?"

I said, "It depends on the case. As you saw on the news, we're busy with the murder trial, but before the trial begins there's a lot of waiting involved. So, if it's a short case ... Is this a divorce matter? A custody dispute?"

She hesitated, as if she thought she should ask for her coat back. "Oh, no, nothing like that. Something criminal, I'm afraid."

At that moment I realized that preparing Carly's defense had awakened my old passion for criminal defense. Perhaps it was an indication that my recovery from depression was close to completion.

She settled into the visitor chair and sighed. "When I was young and idealistic, I did something very foolish, and now it's come to light. I'm afraid it will be the end of my career in politics, which is maybe a good thing, but I'd rather retire on my own terms."

I gave her the same speech about what she should and shouldn't tell me, but she shook her head. "No, I did it, and I don't want to cover it up."

I was about to tell her to start from the beginning, when she did just that.

"When I was nineteen, I was a bit of a radical, as you probably know. I was out to save the world, whatever the cost. I was a member of a group that was violently opposed to big business. We started out as a watchdog group that had as its goal exposing the misdeeds of corporations in an anonymous way. It was a lot like WikiLeaks for corporations."

Jen asked. "Why anonymous?"

"Because we did things that crossed the line."

"For example?" I said.

"Everything I say here is confidential, right?"

"Yes."

"Our schtick involved hacking into a corporation's network and finding incriminating documents. We were very good at it." Although she'd been totally poised up to that point, she began clasping and unclasping her handbag. Anxious.

"How many?" I asked.

"In the group?"

"Yeah."

"Only three. Do you remember the leaked materials showing that Tempura Energy's recorded assets and profits were inflated and in some cases totally nonexistent?"

Jen was already a bit starstruck, and her eyes widened. "That was you?"

Sheridan nodded.

"Before you go further," I said, "know that there are statutes of limitations that might be relevant."

"I know that. I'm not worried about any of the things we leaked. As time went on, we grew a little bigheaded based on the success we were having. We got a little cocky and decided that exposing corporate greed wasn't enough; we wanted to do something about it. So, we did."

She finally wedged the purse between her thigh and the side of the chair, where it wouldn't reveal her nervousness. "We found that a company called Hellton Developers falsified information on an environmental impact report, and, as a result, their permit for a major development south of Crescent City, on the ocean, was granted. They went ahead despite the protests and made millions from it."

"What did you do to them?"

"We had a girl—only sixteen—who was a child prodigy when it came to hacking. She liberated seventy thousand dollars from their coffers in a way that made it seem like an accounting error. They were totally oblivious. We used their own obfuscation tricks against them."

"Didn't the company go bankrupt?" Jen asked.

"It did."

"Was that any of your doing?"

"No. They didn't need any help from us. It was their own mismanagement. My theory is that if you hire people who are willing to commit or overlook fraud, you're probably not getting the best people."

I rubbed the back of my neck. "What did you do with the money?"

"We didn't keep it. Not a penny." She smiled. "We took it and made anonymous contributions to the California Coastal Commission, various land trusts, and some charities."

"When was this?"

"1991."

"If you're thinking that there's no statute of limitations because it's embezzlement," I said, "that's only relevant for public funds. You moved money *into* public funds, not out."

She smoothed her hair. "I understand that, but here's the thing. I mentioned that we made the withdrawal hard to find, but eventually they discovered it. Only a year ago."

"And the clock doesn't start ticking until the crime is discovered."

"Right."

I asked, "Have they offered you a plea deal?"

"They have, but any guilty plea would end my political career, as my opponent, pulling strings behind the scenes, knows. I've decided to roll the dice and go for a jury trial."

"Do you have any reason to believe you'll be acquitted?" I glanced at Jen, and she responded with a micro-nod.

"No."

Back in Courtroom 4, the bailiff called Carly's case. Reporters, as well as citizens with nothing better to do, filled the spectator seats. The drizzly weather resulted in a wet-dog smell from all the damp coats and sweatshirts.

It was the day to argue my motions to suppress two pieces of evidence: the eyewitness testimony and the video recording of Carly's conversation with Bridget. Without the eyewitness testimony, the prosecution had no way to place Carly at the scene of the alleged crime.

Without the conversation, they had nothing suggesting a motive. Proving motive isn't required for a conviction, but it can go a long way toward convincing a jury of the defendant's guilt.

Science warns us not to rely on eyewitness testimony, and yet it is often an important part of the prosecution's case. In 1984, a man by the name of Kirk Bloodsworth was sentenced to death based primarily on the testimony of five eyewitnesses. It was only after he spent six long years in prison waiting for his execution that DNA evidence exonerated him.

In fact, The Innocence Project found that of the cases overturned by DNA analysis, seventy-three percent relied on eyewitness testimony. Testimony that turned out to be wrong. Memory doesn't work like Google Photos, with pictures or videos stored in our brains, available to be reviewed later on. It's more like a jigsaw puzzle, and often the police will supply some of the wrong pieces in order to bolster their case.

Scientists have recommended that the officer conducting any lineup or photo identification session should not be aware of the identity of the suspect, and the witness should be told that the suspect may not be in the lineup. In the real world, those recommendations are rarely followed.

I'd chosen a Harris tweed sport coat, something that might get me thrown out of an LA courtroom, but counted as overdressed in Humboldt. I put two hands on the lectern. "Your Honor, Detective Crawford poisoned this witness the moment he showed her Ms. Romero's photo all by itself. That seared the image into her mind, so that any later photo lineups weren't reliable."

Finn stood. "Our witness is very sure of the ID. She'll testify that there's no question about it."

I turned from Finn to the judge. "She's sure now but not when she made the initial ID. May I read from the court transcript, Your Honor?"

"Yes."

"Let's see. This is from my cross, concerning the photo of the defendant that Detective Crawford showed the witness. 'Question by Mr. Goodlove: How sure were you at that point, when he first showed you the photo? Answer: Well, maybe not so sure then. But I've played it over. In my head. I realized that it was her.'"

I put down the transcript. "Your Honor, that's a textbook example of why many courts now advise jurors to ignore expressions of confidence when listening to witnesses testify."

The judge turned to the prosecution table. "Ms. Finn?"

"Mr. Goodlove is free to discredit the witness at trial."

Stevens nodded. "I agree. I am going to allow the testimony. Mr. Goodlove, I'll ask you to submit jury instructions related to eyewitness testimony, which I will evaluate." She rapped the gavel. "Okay, your next motion concerns … the inadvertently recorded sign-language conversation between Ms. Romero and Ms. Dundon."

Jen handled this one. "Your Honor, California Penal Code Section six thirty-two states that all parties must consent when an electronic recording device is used to eavesdrop upon a confidential communication. The security camera at the coffee shop is a recording device even though it records video and not audio. Also, I'll ask you to imagine the outcry if microphones routinely recorded conversations at coffee shops and other public places. Security cams are tolerated only because sign-language conversations are rare."

"Ms. Finn?"

"Yes, Your Honor. Under the plain view doctrine, if a homeowner leaves his curtains open, he can't expect privacy from someone looking in. In a federal case concerning butt-dialing, the—"

"What dialing?" Judge Stevens's frown brought her eyebrows from their freakishly high position down to something approaching normal.

"I'm sorry, Your Honor. That term refers to inadvertently dialing a number, sometimes nine-one-one, by sitting on your smartphone. When that happens, whoever was called hears your conversations even though you may not realize you are being overheard."

"I did not know that. Please continue." Her lack of knowledge cemented the impression that this dowager had been transported to the twenty-first century from Downton Abbey.

"In that case, the federal judge wrote that, and I'm quoting, 'a person who knowingly operates a device that is capable of inadvertently exposing his conversations to third-party listeners and fails to take simple precautions to prevent such exposure does not have a reasonable expectation of privacy with respect to statements that are exposed to an outsider by the inadvertent operation of that device.'"

"Your Honor," Jen said, "that case is not on point. Neither of the participants was operating the security camera."

Finn almost seemed to whine, sounding desperate. "But their conversation was in plain view, anyone could see it."

Jen shook her head. "But not record it. That would have been illegal."

"The cameras are there to prevent crime, not eavesdrop on conversations, Your Honor." Finn was grasping at straws and not being careful about which straw she grabbed.

"Yes," Jen said, "and that's exactly why the two women, even if they knew the coffee shop had security cameras, had no reasonable expectation their privacy would be violated."

"Thank you, counselors. I am ruling in favor of the defense on this motion. The video may not be introduced or referred to in the trial." She banged her gavel.

Jen and I gathered up our papers. One loss, one win. I whispered in Jen's ear. "Would have been better the other way."

She knew what I meant. With the exclusion of the eyewitness testimony, their case would have been knocked out of the sky like a hot-air balloon hit with the cruise missile. Our exclusion of the video, on the other hand, wouldn't prevent the prosecution from calling Bridget Dundon to testify.

Chapter Eleven

JEN AND I ONCE again found ourselves in Humboldt's largest courtroom, Courtroom 4. The public interest in Isabel Sheridan's trial for grand theft was as great as for Carly's trial, and the spectator area was standing room only. I had rapidly become Humboldt's most famous lawyer, with people recognizing me on the street and potential clients climbing into our office over the transom.

The murmuring crowd contained a few paparazzi, as rare as desert antelopes in the redwood forest. Photos weren't allowed in the courtroom, but I thought maybe they were covertly snapping shots of the beautiful politician. Certainly, they would alert their cohorts outside the courthouse as soon as Sheridan was about to leave.

Our judge was the florid Tipp Theodore, known by his inevitable nickname, Tipsy Ted. Ted was a man with a constant hangover. I was convinced he self-medicated with hair of the dog during recesses. His nose looked like a Ballpark Frank that had plumped until it burst, and his eyebrows suggested he had some Sasquatch in his gene pool.

I pitied him, actually. I rarely drank hard liquor because the next day always came packaged with a twelve-hour hangover, during which I was useless. I'd learned my lesson when I'd defended a drug user—a case in which Finn was the prosecutor, in fact. I'd had too many drinks with an old law school friend the night before, and the resultant hangover took a wrecking ball to my closing arguments. Finn took full advantage of my impairment, but I managed to squeak by with an acquittal. Never again.

Isabel Sheridan's misdeeds had been uncovered during the interminable period of forensic accounting that followed Hellton's bankruptcy. Her fingerprints were all over the fraudulent transactions, and her younger colleague had long since fled the country, continuing her guerrilla hacktivism from an undisclosed location.

The prosecution made the mistake of vilifying our client. *Did they not envision the outcome that Jen and I hoped for?* They also put the jury to sleep by slogging through the complicated accounting wizardry that had uncovered the deeds of the activists.

They recounted the nefarious techniques Ms. Sheridan and her "gang" had used to escape detection: moving from place to place, wardriving, illegally piggybacking on the networks of unsuspecting homeowners.

Tipsy Ted sent some suspicious looks my way, definitely suspecting our strategy. As long as we were careful, we'd escape any sanctions.

Our expert accountant testified that every penny of the money fraudulently withdrawn from the company, including interest, was transferred by Sheridan's outlaw group to the charities representing interests most harmed by Hellton Developers. In addition, Ms. Sheridan had, before her crime was discovered, contributed to the Hellton liquidation fund in the amount of $70,000. She did that anonymously, but we were able to show that the contribution came from her account. Bottom line, she didn't keep any money from the embezzlement, and she used her own funds to help those who'd lost their investments in Hellton.

We put our client on the stand, where she shone. *Would Carly do as well as a witness?* You might have thought it was Keira Knightly up on the stand based on the reaction of the crowd. They sat spellbound as she admitted her crime. She didn't express remorse as much as convey that it had been a stupid thing to do.

The prosecutor pounced on her lack of remorse, even though we'd preemptively minimized the effects of such an attack with our demonstration that she'd made restitution in her secretive way. "How long were you in this gang?" he asked.

"Four years."

"And how do we know that you haven't committed other crimes that have not come to light?"

"Objection. Argumentative and beyond the scope of direct."

"Sustained." The ADA got his point across to the jury, however. Perhaps this beautiful woman wasn't as innocent as she seemed. She'd confessed when they caught her, but who knew what evil lurked in her heart?

When the case was given to the jurors, Sheridan, Jen, and I walked to the Lost Coast Brewery and Cafe, two blocks from the courthouse. I had some raw oysters, Jen had a coffee, and Ms. Sheridan went to the women's room to throw up.

When she returned, having lost some of her perpetual tan, she asked, "How can you stand the suspense, the tension? Do you get used to it?"

I shook my head. "No. You learn to deal with it, but it's always there. Like a houseguest who has overstayed his welcome." Lousy analogy. I guess I was a bit tongue-tied. Jen frowned and looked at me sideways. Like, *What's with the boss today?*

After lunch, we took a walk down Redwood Point's boardwalk. Not boards, but cement scored to look like wood. It was deserted, as usual. Envisioned as a gathering place, it functioned mostly as a place for homeless people to nap. Sheridan stopped to talk to a few of them—they probably thought they were dreaming.

On the hike back to our office, I got the call that the jury had reached a verdict. I never speculate about whether a quick deliberation was good for the prosecution or the defense. It's no more productive than picking petals off a daisy: The jury loves me; the jury loves me not.

We were mobbed when we approached the courthouse. As a politician, Sheridan innately understood the concept of "no comment."

We all rose as the jurors entered the room. Several of them looked at Sheridan as they filed into the jury box.

Judge Theodore cleared his throat. "Has the jury reached a verdict?"

"We have, sir."

"Would you please hand that verdict to the bailiff?"

When the judge got the folded-over sheet, he held it close to his face, going over it. "Okay. The Court has reviewed the verdict form and finds it in order. I'm going to hand it to the court clerk, Ms. Beacon, who will publish the verdict."

Ms. Beacon stood. "The Superior Court of California, Humboldt County. The people of the State of California, plaintiff, versus Isabel Rachel Sheridan, defendant. Case number CR 2987721. We, the jury in the above-entitled action, find the defendant, Isabel Rachel Sheridan, not guilty of the crime of grand theft in violation of Penal Code Section four eight seven ..."

Ms. Sheridan squeezed my hand. I reached for the airplane sickness bag in my briefcase, but she didn't need it.

She hugged me and then Jen. "Thank you both."

The judge gave me a dirty look before cracking his gavel and dismissing the jury.

Jury nullification was what we'd been hoping for, and it's what we got. The courts like to keep it under wraps, but a jury is free to bring back a not guilty verdict even when they believe that a law was broken. That is, they cannot be penalized for saying, "Sure, the defendant is guilty, but screw that, we're going to acquit him. Or her."

I'd watched the jurors when the judge read the relevant part of the jury instructions, namely: *You must follow the law exactly as I give it to you, even if you disagree with it.*

Such a strange thing. Jurors are lied to by the judge. They're told they must decide based only on the law, something that's not true. The example that's often given is that of a suitor who uses his key to sneak into his girlfriend's house and add a fortune cookie to the cookie jar. The confection holds an engagement ring, with which he intends to surprise her. Upon hearing unsettling noises from the bedroom, he goes in and interrupts his bride-no-longer-to-be *in flagrante delicto*. Arguments ensue, and the girlfriend kicks the unhappy suitor out of the house, demanding his key. The suitor then remembers the ring, breaks in, and takes it back. Despite clear evidence of breaking and entering, jurors might feel they don't agree with the law in that case and acquit the defendant.

That was the result we'd hoped for, and the jury came through. If I'd even hinted that they could ignore the judge's instructions during the trial, I'd have been in trouble, but somehow the message got through.

The judge can do nothing to change the verdict. When it goes the other way, if the jury convicts the defendant despite a clear lack of evidence of guilt, the judge can give a directed verdict of not guilty. That situation, known as "jury vilification" is rare. Jury nullification, however, is much more common than most realize.

The three of us, Jen, Sheridan, and I, went back to the office and celebrated with a hot fire and a cold bottle of champagne.

* * *

I was at a coffee shop in an armchair, reading the news on my phone when something—*a bug?*—tickled the top of my ear. I flicked it with a finger and kept reading. It happened again, but that second time, I knew it was no bug. Fool me twice and all that. But I didn't let on, flapping again as if totally absorbed in my reading. Someone nearby giggled. The third time I was ready.

When it came, I snapped my hand up, grabbed the offending fingers, and held on.

"*Ow!*" Sibyl Finn tried to pull her hand back.

I kept my grip. "I think there was a spider on my ear. Were you trying to save me?"

"C'mon, Garrett, let go." She was smiling now, and I imagined pulling her hand until she dropped into my lap.

"No, it could be one of those wolf spiders. Maybe it's already bitten us. We'd better go outside before I let go."

She'd tied her flaming hair back in a ponytail, exposing the delicate lines of her neck and a soft earlobe decorated with a shamrock earring.

What the hell. I pulled her hand across my body, and her butt fell squarely into the center of my lap. She yelped with a non-prosecutorial squeal. The maneuver would have been perfectly executed had I not knocked my travel mug onto the floor. No worries; it didn't leak.

Finn started to get up. "I don't think—"

I held her in place. "No. Whatever you do, don't get up. The venom will make the blood rush to the wound and you'll pass out."

"If there's any blood rushing somewhere, it's not mine."

"Oh my God!" I whispered.

She crossed her arms, staying where she was but twisting to look me in the eye. "Now what?"

I pointed at her hair, a grimace of horror on my face. "Was it that color before the spider bit you?"

Shaking her head, she yanked her fingers free, stood, then bent over and picked up my travel mug. I reached for it, but she pulled it away, a twinkle in her eyes. "I think you've already had too much caffeine."

She dropped into the armchair next to mine. "I swear, Garrett, this is a side of you I haven't seen since—for a while."

I put my fingers on my wrist, as if checking my pulse. "Must be the venom."

Of course it wasn't the imagined venom or the caffeine that was bumping my heart rate. It was suddenly seeing this exotic Miss Ireland as something other than opposing counsel. She wore a fuzzy cashmere sweater that matched her hair and emphasized her curves. When she was on my lap, her wool slacks had accentuated her soft yet firm derriere—*she work out?*—adding more beats per minute to my palpitations.

"If you're done embarrassing us in public, Mr. Goodlove, I'm going to grab a bite at the smokehouse." She tilted her head toward the restaurant across the street. Her voice and manner revealed nothing but confidence. No hesitancy or sheepish smile. It was as if she'd casually mentioned that her car was blue. But she had a tell: A flush crept up her cheeks. She put her hand to her face.

"Well, counselor," I said, "I'll have to think back to my ethics course. Dating opposing counsel. Hmm."

"Dating? Who said anything about dating? Ah, it's because we" —bunny quotes— "held hands. That it?"

I looked around with a confused frown. "Someone here was sitting in my lap. I thought it was you."

"Yeah, right. Ha ha."

"I thank you for your offer, Madam Prosecutor, but unfortunately I have other plans for dinner. Besides, I don't want people to think that 'Tickle my ear, and I'll follow you anywhere' works with me."

Her blush still in place, she said goodbye with a wink and a smile. I watched her through the window as she walked across the street but ducked my head down when she looked back. *What was happening?* A song ran through my mind, and I rubbed my forehead trying to place it. I hummed it. *Ah, Billy Joel's "For the Longest Time."* Right, this was something that hadn't happened for the longest time.

Louella knocked on the open door to my office and walked in. "Ready for your walk, boy?"

"You're not serious." I was huddled with my laptop by the fire in my office. The ancient radiators were not cutting it on that stormy February day. The rain suddenly rattled against the window panes, and I pointed as if I'd planned that gust in order to make my point. "That's bad, bad weather out there."

"No such thing as bad weather, just bad clothing."

"You've been reading the LL Bean catalog again."

"Come on, let's go. It looks much worse from in here. We can get some oysters at Jack's Seafood. Your treat."

Louella is what I call a walk-talker. She likes to walk while discussing things, unlike me. I made one more hopeful gesture toward the warm fire, but she didn't go for it.

I put on my Northface jacket, which counted as good clothing for my upper body, but my legs were protected by nothing more than business slacks. "Guess I should have worn my long johns today."

Looking at my legs, she shook her head. "Let's stop by my house."

Her coat came down to her ankles. It was thick with a floral pattern on the outside, fur on the inside, and a hood. She pulled the drawstring on her hood, and we walked down The Pink Lady's steps. That was the nickname for the Victorian building that housed my office.

"Are you ready to be brought up to speed?" she asked.

"Brr!"

"Okay then. I've found that both Angelo Romero and Wenzel Rozetti, the crabber, have some connection with a telemarketing company called DialUSA. It's out in Blue Lake."

"Big company?" A gust of rain-filled wind soaked my pants.

"No, small."

"And Rozetti said he didn't know Angelo, right?"

"Yes. He's probably telling the truth. Rozetti was just a lowly employee, like I was for two days." She filled me in on her temporary job with DialUSA. "But I don't know what Angelo's connection was. He definitely didn't just make phone calls. I think he was involved with their sketchy activities."

"Sketchy as in illegal?"

"Pretty much." She led me into her house. The place was neat, but the cigarette odor was overpowering. If I were king, I'd make them illegal. She stubbed out her current cancer stick in an ashtray and opened a heavy wood chest in the hall.

A new smell, the odor of mothballs, made me feel as if we'd just been crop dusted. "Jeez, Louella. No one uses mothballs anymore. I feel like I'm at my grandmother's house."

Without comment she rummaged around and pulled out a thick men's coat. Wool? It made me think of 1930s mobsters in a Chicago winter. She held it up.

"Now I know you're joking," I said.

"It was my husband's. Put it on. Let's go. Here, put this on, too." She handed me a yellow oilskin cap.

"Were you married to Captain Ahab?"

That got a tiny huff of a laugh from her as she lit up her next cigarette. I needed to get some fresh air, so I humored her, shaking the coat to try to eliminate some of the pesticide odor before putting my arms into the sleeves and shrugging it on.

Back in the rain, I resumed our conversation. "Sketchy how?"

"I think the telemarketing part is a front for criminal activity. We know Angelo seemed to be a slimy guy. Not on the up-and-up."

"Yeah. I've confirmed that with Carly." I tightened the strap on the sailor hat. "Is it telephone fraud?"

"Looks like it. I'm still pursuing it."

We came to the waterfront and started south on the cement boardwalk. Whitecaps filled the harbor, and no boats were out. The barks of sea lions drifted to us in the gusts, the rain making no difference to them.

"That's good," I said. "If we can show that he was involved in criminal activity, especially organized crime, it will give the jury reasonable doubt as to who killed him."

"It's looking a lot like organized crime. Let me tell you what happened a few nights ago."

We had arrived at Jack's Seafood on the boardwalk. I started for the door, but Louella held me back.

Despite the hundred-pound coat, I was cold. "Let's go in, and you can tell me."

"Hold on. A few nights ago, I was putting groceries in my car. I was leaning into the trunk when a guy comes out of nowhere. I must be losing my touch; I didn't see him come up to me. He said, 'You better start minding your own business, grandma.'"

"Shit. Louella!"

"Don't worry. I spun around and had my gun in his nose before he knew what hit him. I pushed it, and I think I cut a nostril open, then I stepped back. He turned and ran."

"You didn't shoot."

"No. I couldn't be sure of a proper backstop. I could have hit someone else."

"Once a cop …"

"Right," she said.

"Did you notify the police?"

She shrugged. "I decided not to. I doubt they could find him, but more importantly, it would tip our hand, right?"

"Do you think this was related to Angelo?"

"I hope so." She led the way into the restaurant, and I followed. "Isn't it nice when the bad guys tell you you're on the right track?" That was one way of looking at it.

The waitress sat us in a booth with a view of the harbor. The family in the neighboring booth moved to a different table. Their kid held his nose.

"Sorry," I called out. *Louella and her stupid mothballs!*

"Garrett, you be careful with Finn, okay?"

"What do you mean?"

Louella put on her reading glasses and scanned the menu. "She's sneaky. I wouldn't trust her as far as I can throw her. And you should know how far you can throw her."

"I'm losing the thread here, Lou."

She turned the page of the menu, not looking up. "You threw her into your lap, from what I heard, then did some major ogling of her ass. I think I'm going to have the shrimp cocktail."

Chapter Twelve

JEN STOPPED HER PACING and stamped the floor so hard I thought she might injure her foot. "Damn it, Garrett, a jury consultant can make all the difference."

Jen and I were having our biggest disagreement yet. I sat in a maroon leather Queen Anne chair in her office, while she stomped around.

"It works, maybe," I said, "but at what cost?"

"You're worried about the cost? How much is your sister's freedom worth to you?"

I leaned forward, my muscles tensing. "That's not a fair question. We have a limited amount we can spend. We've already blown through the rainy day fund. Carly is borrowing, and I've put a second mortgage on my house. I've had to pay top dollar for expert witnesses that Finn won't tear apart: DNA, ocean current, eyewitness reliability—"

"At least talk to the consultant."

"How much does she charge?"

Jen dropped into the chair behind her desk and mumbled something.

"Speak up."

"A hundred thousand."

"What would we get for that?"

She pulled a pen from the jar and started tapping it on her blotter. "The basic juror ranking, and one mock trial. And a shadow jury."

The consultant would put together a test jury, like a focus group, and we could test our arguments, ask them if they were convincing. Then she'd put together a shadow jury that had a similar makeup to the one seated, and we could get their feedback along the way.

"Right. I've used consultants in the past, and I haven't been impressed."

"Yeah, well things are different now." She leaned back in her chair and put her stockinged feet on the desk.

"How?"

"Two words: 'social' and 'media.'"

I opened my mouth then closed it. She was right. There was, in reality, no such thing as privacy in this modern world, and most people's beliefs and biases could be uncovered with a few clicks.

Jen saw her opening. "Let me show you the presentation video."

I got up and stood behind her as she brought up A3 Consulting's website.

"Ready?"

"Ready."

The video started with a slick logo, a professional drawing of two huge hands pulling jurors out of the jury box by the scruffs of their necks.

I laughed. "Nice image."

Next, the firm's head, Lana Thomas, stood in a courtroom, her arms crossed. She struck me as ultraserious and perhaps a little arrogant.

"Trials can be won or lost even before the opening statements," she said. "Our AI analysis of prospective jurors ranks them on a multidimensional matrix that is frighteningly accurate when it comes to predicting their reaction to your well-crafted arguments. With our mock trials, you can try out your narrative, improving your arguments and your communication based on the responses of the shadow jury. In litigation, the best narrative wins. The shadow juries can give you feedback along the way and allow you to make midcourse corrections."

We finished the smooth presentation, and Jen looked up at me.

I leaned on her desk. "She's good, I admit that."

"But?"

"But I don't agree that the best narrative wins. I give the jurors credit for deciding based on the facts, and if we present them well, we have a chance."

"You used to say that whichever lawyer they like better wins."

I bobbled my head side to side. "Well, that's important, too. And that's different from narrative, of course. Number one, facts. Number two, likability—we have to be more likable than Finn, which won't be easy. A distant third is the narrative, the story we tell about how the facts string together." I gestured to her computer screen. "That consultant doesn't come off as very likable, by the way. Sure, the hundred K might give us a ten percent advantage, or it may not help at all."

She leaned back and took a deep breath. "Okay. You may be right."

I raised my eyebrows and made a rolling gesture with my hand.

"What?" She smiled. "Sir?"

"As ..."

She frowned and cocked her head.

"As usual," I said.

She gave a laugh that lit up her face. "Very funny."

I gave her my hand and pulled her up into a hug. *What prompted that?* "Jen, I appreciate that you care so much, as if Carly were your sister, too. It'll be fine. We're going to win this thing." *Do I really believe that?*

I needed a break from lawyering and decided to play private detective for a day. Why should Louella have all the fun? I checked with her to make sure we weren't duplicating effort and then headed out to find out more about Angelo's supposed tattoo.

Carly had said that he was anti-tattoo, and she definitely hadn't seen one on the back of his neck. But they'd been separated for a year before he died. I checked with some bartenders, and two confirmed that they'd seen the tattoo. Angelo was showing it off to everyone, apparently.

I was astounded to find nine tattoo parlors in Redwood Point, and when I visited them, I was even more shocked at some of the things people had permanently inked onto their bodies. Each shop had a wall of photos. The most surprising was a woman's arm tattooed with a naked girl being explicitly fondled by a skeleton in a black cloak. Another had a stamp image on her breast: *USDA Inspected for Wholesomeness.* The photo also revealed the breast implant scar, but I wasn't judging.

There were a lot of designs with nautical themes: orcas, jellyfish, dolphins, squids, and Ursula from Disney's *The Little Mermaid*. No sharks.

The fifth shop I visited looked like a cross between a barbershop and a hospital room, with gurneys instead of barber chairs. The walls were bloodred, the floor had a black-and-white checkerboard pattern, and the lights were dim.

I spoke to a muscular woman with half her body, the right half, filled with ink. "Have you done any shark tattoos here?"

"I don't work here, friend."

A biker type came out of the back, drying his hands on a paper towel. "How can I help you?"

"I'd like to find out whether you've done any shark tattoos recently."

"Hey, I don't rat out anybody, man. You a cop?"

I should have left this to Louella. I smiled. "There's no ratting out involved, I promise you. I'm trying to find out what happened to someone. He had a new tattoo on the back of his neck. A shark with blood around it." The tattoo information hadn't gotten into the news. I slipped him a twenty.

"What's this for?"

"For your time."

"Nah. Keep it. Let me check with my partner. He did some fish thing." The biker guy went into the back and returned in less than a minute. "Nah, he did a pair of moray eels on a guy's butt. They were coming out of a hole, if you get my drift." He gave a hearty laugh, and the muscle woman joined in.

"So, no sharks?"

He shook his head.

"Okay, thanks. Let me know if you hear about any shark tattoos." I left my card and dropped the twenty into the tip jar on my way out.

I checked every other parlor in town, although two had gone out of business. No luck. Back at the office, Jen suggested that maybe he went out of town to get it done.

"Why would he do that?"

"Beats me, but if you want to be thorough …"

"You're suggesting a road trip?"

She kept her deadpan expression but jiggled her eyebrows. "Overnight stay?"

"If you think you can keep your hands off me."

She scoffed a little harder than I would have liked. We started Googling tattoo parlors in Redding. The phone rang.

I answered. "Goodlove and Shek."

"Hey, man. That shark tattoo. I found out who did it."

Angelo had had it done at one of the parlors that had recently shut its doors. Jen and I went to the home of the woman who'd done the artwork, a short twenty-something with a buzz cut.

"Yeah, I remember him." She stood in her doorway and didn't invite us in. "He said he didn't care what the design was, he just wanted it to be recognizable."

"What do you think he meant?" I asked.

"How the hell should I know? All I know is that he said he didn't want some abstract shit. I said, 'How about a tiger or a lion?' He's like, 'How about a shark?' And that's what I did. By the way, the police called me right after the guy was croaked. Someone told them he had a tattoo, and they called all the parlors."

"And when did he get the tattoo?"

"I remember because it was my birthday. November twenty-second."

Just a week and a half before he died.

Hiking in the redwoods, Carly and I took a lunch break. We climbed onto a log the size of a semitruck and pulled out Subway sandwiches and beer.

Comparisons between a redwood forest and a cathedral are right on the money. Both have huge pillars, high ceilings, and complete silence. Birdsong is rare; the trees are resistant to insects, and fewer insects means fewer birds. The duff on the ground—a thick layer of fragrant needles, leaves, and twigs—further absorbed most sounds. The light was low because storm clouds were blowing in from the ocean.

We ate without communicating, each lost in our own thoughts.

Carly finished first, packing the sandwich wrapping into her backpack and balancing her beer on the uneven bark of the decaying log. "Have you checked up on Toby?"

Damn. It had slipped my mind. "Not yet."

"You forgot."

I said nothing.

"Remember Great-aunt Laurie."

Good point. Our great-aunt Laurie had graduated high school as valedictorian then started acting strange in her first year at Cornell. She was diagnosed with bipolar disorder, called manic depression back then. She swung between exhilarating episodes of overachieving to days when she couldn't get out of bed. I'd met her only once, at a time when her medication was keeping her on an even but suppressed keel.

"Carly, there's something I need to disclose to you. You know that Finn and I have been friends for years, despite being opponents in court."

"You want to have sex with her." She used the more vulgar sign for "have sex," the one that looks to me like two bunny rabbits bumping each other.

"No. Come on. Why do you say that?"

"You two were fooling around at Starbucks."

What? Was it televised or something? "We were just kidding around."

"That's what I said."

"Okay. Well, anyway, if we have any kind of relationship, I need to tell you, and that's what I'm doing now."

"Is it love or lust?" Leave it to Carly to ask insightful questions.

I thought about it. Thunder rumbled in the west. Carly was oblivious to it.

"Well?"

"Ach. I don't really know, okay? I wouldn't even be thinking about this if I didn't have an ethical obligation to tell you. So, is it okay if it turns out we have some kind of thing? Actually, I will probably stay away from her, socially, until after the trial is over, but I needed to tell you."

"It's a good thing, isn't it?" She looked me in the eyes.

"What do you mean?"

"If she falls in love with you, it will be hard for her to convict your twin sister, right?"

Had I been thinking that when I pulled Finn into my lap?

I listened to the thunder, which was getting closer. "Let's head back to the car. It's about to start raining."

The next morning, I swung by Toby's apartment. My knock was answered by his roommate, a teenager with a mullet and a Southern accent to match. I looked behind him into the apartment. Pizza boxes on the coffee table, beer bottles on the floor, and ripped couch cushions. The usual. Trying to get Toby to clean up his room had been a constant battle when he lived at home. It wasn't my problem anymore.

"Not here, dude." The roommate called everyone dude. "He's out taking photos."

"Do you know where?"

"Yeah, dude. Out on the jetty."

I nodded. "How's he doing?"

"Who, Toby?"

No, Prince Harry. Sheesh. "Yeah."

He shrugged. "Okay, I guess."

"Any ups and downs?"

"What?"

"Does his mood tend to fluctuate? Up and down?"

"I guess." He shrugged again. "No, not really, dude. Sometimes he just kinda hangs out around here."

"Okay, thanks."

Walking back to the car, I texted my son: *Where you at?*

It wasn't until I'd gotten back to the office that I got the reply: *North Jetty.*

Meet you there.

Cool.

To get to the ocean from Redwood Point Harbor, ships must cross over the treacherous "bar" between two jetties. In the 1800s, ten percent of the lumber boats attempting it wrecked. Nowadays, in winter, ships often have to wait weeks for the swell to be manageable enough to allow a crossing. The jetties themselves are dangerous, with rogue waves that seem eager to pull unsuspecting tourists into the sea.

The swell was running high when I parked in the sand lot by the north jetty. Waves whooshed along the rocks in turn, sounding like 747s passing over the end of a runway. Carly had surfed here with her friends many times. Not me. Too gnarly.

As I feared, Toby was far out on the jetty, squatting down, presumably taking photographs. *That kid has no common sense.* I waved, but he wasn't looking my way. The smell of a dead animal occasionally washed over me with the stronger gusts. Probably a seal carcass on the beach. I was halfway to him when he turned, waved, and started my way.

People often say, "Never, *ever* turn your back on the ocean." I always think, *And if you're in Kansas?* But the advice made sense in this situation, and Toby was unaware of the big set that was rolling in behind him. His clothing already soaked, he should have known to keep a weather eye out.

I waved both hands over my head, but his attention was focused on choosing his foot placements. The largest of the waves passed the metal tower at the tip of the jetty, the automated structure that stood in for a real lighthouse. The wave covered the rocks as it progressed, like God's firehose spraying retardant foam. I yelled. No way could he hear me.

Finally, the sound of the approaching breaker caught his attention. He dropped into a crevice between two dolosse, huge cement structures that looked like Paul Bunyan's toy jacks. Toby disappeared when the wave washed over him. When it passed, he popped up, giving me a big thumbs up. Even from where I was, his smile stood out. The next, bigger wave hit him, and he fell forward.

He popped back up a little more slowly that time and looked seaward. *I guess he can learn.* When we met, he was shivering like a Chihuahua at the North Pole. His forehead sported a two-inch gash surrounded by road rash that resembled a scraped pizza. *Did he even know he was cut?*

I said, "What the *hell* is wrong with—" *Stop! Not helpful.*

My abusive comment put only a momentary dent in his smile. "It's okay, Dad. Check this out. It's a dry bag. The camera's fine." He unsnapped and unrolled the screaming-orange bag and pointed to the Nikon inside, surrounded with bubble wrap.

"Aren't you cold?" The gusts were whipping by us, and I had to raise my voice to be heard. He wore only jeans and an O'Neill hoodie that Carly had given him. We jogged back to my car. I got him inside, turned the heat on high, and pulled the first aid kit and some emergency clothing from the trunk. I got him to exchange his soaking shirt and sweatshirt for a wool sweater and a foil emergency blanket. If anything, his shivering got worse.

"Dad, I've got to show you these shots I got." He swiped through the shots on his camera and handed it to me. "Check this out. That's the best one."

It was good. Not worth dying for, but good. The wave had a pipeline curl, just about to crash on the tip of the jetty.

"And check out the gulls. What a rush, right?"

The seagulls were lit by the rays of the morning sun and stood out against the dark clouds behind them.

I sighed. "It's a great shot, buddy, but what if one of those waves had knocked you off the jetty? Did you even think about that when you went out there?"

"That's part of the excitement, don't you think? I've never felt so alive. Did you see that wave knock me over? Wow."

On cue, the gash in his forehead started bleeding more. I cleaned it up, spread some Neosporin on it, and applied a bandage from the first aid kit.

Toby didn't stop talking. Mania or just an exuberant twenty year old? I'm not a shrink, but I decided on the latter.

I interrupted his chatter. "Toby, Aunt Carly said you went to her house in the middle of the night and started going through her books. What was that all about?"

"When?"

I pushed gauze against some small, oozing cuts above his eyebrows. "Two weeks after Uncle Angelo died."

"Oh, yeah. I remember. I knew I'd seen something that gave me a great idea for a photo shoot, but I couldn't quite think what it was. You know, like tip of the tongue. Then I realized that it came from a book at Carly's, so I went over there and went through the books. It was late at night, and I didn't want to wake her up."

"It wouldn't have kept until morning?"

"Creativity, you know what I mean? I couldn't take a chance that I'd forget."

Where does creativity end and mental illness begin? I've often thought some artists—Christo and his wrapping of bridges in yellow sheets, for example—were crazy, just in an entertaining way.

I decided, however, that there was no conclusive evidence my son needed help. Not yet, anyway. Maybe I'd revisit the idea after the trial.

Chapter Thirteen

LOUELLA WAS MAKING PROGRESS. Her two goals were to get a feeling for Angelo and to uncover his ties to any organized crime syndicate that had its fingers in the DialUSA pie.

On a Monday afternoon, the Forest Grove Bar and Grill was closed, and the bartender, a tiny woman with blonde hair and dark eyebrows, announced that fact when Louella walked in.

"Sorry, ma'am, we're closed."

Louella glanced at a scruffy old man leaning over a beer in a back booth. The lights chased out any class that the place may have held at night, exposing the dirt in the cracks of the wood floor and the dust on the bottles. Every inch of space was filled with flasks, stickers, neon signs, and posters. An elk head looked ready to fall off the wall behind the bar, and the stale beer scent managed to overpower Louella's impaired sense of smell.

She climbed onto a barstool. "I just have a few questions."

"I'm Cindy. What'll you have?"

So much for being closed. Louella looked over the bottles. "Uh … how about a Jagerade?"

Cindy turned and grabbed the green Jägermeister flask from the shelf and a bottle of Gatorade from the fridge. She mixed drinks for both of them. "Hip hooray for electrolytes." She had a black leather apron, a lumberjack shirt, and a forearm covered with tattoos.

"Did you know Angelo Romero?" Louella asked.

"*Oh* yeah. He was a regular here. Until his wife pushed him off the cliff."

"You think his wife did it?"

"Well, I don't know." Cindy pulled a wooden stool over and sat on it. "I guess that's what you're trying to figure out. I just know that if I was his wife, I'd kill him."

"Why's that?"

"He was here most nights. You wouldn't even know he was married from the way he acted."

"How much do you know about him?"

"Pretty much, actually. A lot of nights he got drunk, poured out his troubles to me, and closed the place out. At first, he was trying to get into my pants, but later he just wanted to talk."

"What was he like?"

"Most people saw him as a sleazeball, but he was kind of sweet inside. When he was drunk, anyway. I think he tried to do the right thing, but he was ambitious. He was always thinking of ways to make a quick buck. You know the type."

Louella sipped her drink, letting Cindy fill the silence.

"You know those phone scams you hear about? Identity theft, that kind of thing? He laughed about those, and I think maybe he was involved or something."

"Sounds pretty sleazy to me."

The bartender poured herself a whiskey. "Yeah, I don't know."

"Did he talk about his wife? How things were between them?"

"No, not at all. They were separated. He didn't talk about her. They were all over with. He was having an affair. At least one."

"Do you know who with?"

Cindy shook her head. "He never came here with her. But, you know, there were two things that were weird."

"Yeah?"

"Yeah. The first thing is that he didn't come in here for two weeks. In November. Then he comes back, and you know why he wasn't here?"

"Why's that?"

"He'd gone on some long trip. He told me about it. Ready for this? First he goes to South Point on the Big Island."

"Hawaii?"

"Right."

"Then to Havasu, you know where that is?"

Louella shrugged. "Somewhere like Arizona."

"Yeah, I think so. Then he went to someplace called La Kay something in Mexico."

"Hold on." Louella took out her phone. "La Paz?"

"No."

"Martínez de la Torre?"

"No, no. Just la something."

"La Quebrada?"

Cindy snapped her fingers. "Yeah, yeah. That's it."

"He say why? Why he went on that trip?"

"Not really." She finished her drink. "I pressed him, 'cause it was weird, right? He just said he was, like, going to grad school, but that didn't make sense."

"What was the second thing?"

Cindy looked at the ceiling. "Second thing ... oh, yeah, before he went, he was nervous. About something. He wouldn't tell me what. I think the cops were onto him. He wasn't relaxed like usual."

Louella worked the gold mine for another hour, left her card and a tip, and headed home. After a nap, she decided she was done burning shoe leather for the day and let her fingers do the walking. The walking took place on her computer keyboard and her phone's dial pad.

She saved the best for last, calling an old contact in the FBI.

"Benson."

"Jeez, they haven't kicked you out yet?"

"Badger! It's been—what—ten years?"

"But you still know my voice." She turned her office chair around and put her feet on an ottoman. Her husband had always kidded her about her ottoman fetish. She had at least twelve of the things.

Benson laughed. "I figured it was either you or Henry Kissinger. A few more years, and your voice will be so low humans won't be able to hear it. What are you doing these days?"

They caught up and discussed the hate-crime murder they'd worked on together.

It's now or never. "I'm working on something the FBI might be involved in. Could you—"

"Sorry, Louella. The answer is no. You should know that."

"Hold on. I have something you guys might be interested in. Here's what I'll do. I'll give you the names of a company and a person, you ask around, and if someone is working on that, tell them I have something for them."

"Why don't you just tell me what you found?"

"Come on, Benson. Are you getting soft in your old age?" She took a drag on her cigarette.

"Right," he said. "You want to trade. Okay, what are the names?"

"DialUSA and Angelo Romero."

An hour after the call, her doorbell rang. She accessed the door camera and saw a tall man with a military haircut and a black windbreaker. He was alert yet relaxed.

She pressed the intercom button. "May I help you?"

"Special Agent Randolph Tick, ma'am, from the FBI." He held his ID up to the camera.

"Just a minute, Agent Tick, I won't be long." She redialed her buddy Benson, who confirmed that her visitor was legit.

She went down the stairs and opened the door. She poked her head out and looked up and down the street. "Come on in. I hope you didn't let anyone follow you here."

"We're good." He walked behind her up the stairs. "Benson said you had some information."

She sat at her desk, lit up a cigarette, and offered him one. He shook his head.

"Is that all he told you?"

"He said you wanted to trade, but I'm not authorized to tell you very much."

"I don't need much."

"What have you got?" he asked.

She told him about the back room at DialUSA. "I overheard a conversation. Here's what I'd like to know: What kind of outfit are we dealing with here, and what was Angelo Romero's involvement with it?"

"Is that all?"

"It's not much, is it? His wife is accused of killing him, and I just want to know whether there are some heavies who might have done it. Whatever else you've got, I don't care about it. Hopefully, Benson has already vouched for me." She raised her eyebrows and tilted her head forward.

"He has."

"Figured. So let me know if this might have been a mob hit or whatever, and I'll tell you what I heard."

"You working for the widow's lawyer?" he asked.

Louella nodded.

Tick got up and walked to the window. He looked out for a while then came back. "Okay. I don't know anything about Angelo Romero, but yes, DialUSA is involved with organized crime. That's all I can tell you."

"Fair enough. Here's what I heard." She described the conversation. "That helpful to you?"

Agent Tick waggled his hand. "It confirms some things, so that helps. You didn't get a look at the technical guy, the guy you said sounded smaller."

"No."

"Okay," he said. "But that he came from Ferndale is good info. Maybe that's the best part. That lets us narrow things down a little."

"I'm curious about what they're doing. Guess you don't want to share?"

He shook his head.

"Want to hear what I think?"

"Yeah."

"I think they record someone talking, maybe during a telemarketing call, then they use some computer wizardry to make that voice say anything they want it to say. They use that to scam money from friends or family members of the owner of that voice."

Tick laughed. "You've got an active imagination, Ms. Davis."

She looked at him. His laugh seemed forced.

At the door, Agent Tick stopped. "Ms. Davis, these are bad people we're dealing with. Benson said you can take care of yourself, and I don't have to tell you that you should be careful."

"No, Agent Tick, you don't need to tell me that. Thank you for coming by."

Three long months after the preliminary hearing, it was time for the trial. By the second day of jury selection I was regretting that I hadn't taken Jen's advice and hired a jury consultant. We'd already used three of our peremptory challenges, and Finn had only used one. In baseball terms, we were behind in the count.

Something was wrong with the heating system, and Courtroom 4 was sweltering. It felt as if we'd been transported to the Deep South before air-conditioning. Judge Stevens suffered the most in her black robes. Despite fanning herself with a manila folder, tiny drops of sweat occasionally slid down her high-class forehead. One made it all the way to the tip of her nose.

Any number of jurors can be eliminated for cause—that is, for being incapable of rendering a fair verdict uninfluenced by bias. For example, if a juror states she's been harassed by the police, the prosecution might ask that she be excused for cause. She has a bias that could prevent her from being impartial.

An example was Juror 10, a woman who was large enough to come from another planet. Ms. Rosemary Dawson made no attempt to keep any of her Facebook data private. That information was fair game as long as we didn't friend the person to unearth private details. Passive data mining was okay. Active, not so much.

Ms. Dawson's posts demonstrated a clear law-and-order bias, and during voir dire, I'd been able to elicit some pro-police responses.

"Your Honor," I said, "I would like to excuse Ms. Dawson for cause."

My number one goal in jury selection is to get unfavorable jurors eliminated *for cause*. Striking a juror for cause doesn't cost a thing. While we can eliminate a juror for no stated reason, known as a peremptory challenge, those challenges are limited and therefore precious. In the worst case scenario, we could run out of peremptory challenges and end up with a juror who is both persuasive and destructive but who can't be removed for cause.

In the case of Ms. Dawson, Judge Stevens thought about it for a while, then went through the charade that's all too common in jury selection.

"Ms. Dawson," she said, "do you think you can put aside your feelings about law enforcement and listen to all the evidence and be impartial and fair?"

"Yes, I think I can do that."

It was a farce because scientific studies have shown that the answer to that question, so often asked, was not reliable. Even putting aside the tendency of *Homo sapiens* to be unaware of their biases, the potential jurors might lie if they want to get on the jury. The humongous Ms. Dawson might be champing at the bit to get on the jury and strike her blow for truth, justice, and the American way.

I stood. "May I approach, Your Honor?"

When Finn joined me in front of the bench, I said, "Your Honor, Ms. Dawson has a clear bias here. There's no way she can be impartial."

"She feels that she can put aside her partiality."

I pushed out my lower lip and blew out a breath that would have fluttered my bangs if I'd had any.

Stormy Stevens sent me a scowl.

Watch it, Garrett.

"Your Honor," Finn said, "the defense wants to eliminate anyone who doesn't view RPPD as a snake pit of fascist pigs. Next thing you know—"

"That's enough, Ms. Finn!"

The storm clouds had broken, and Stormy Stevens lived up to her nickname. Lightning bolts leapt from her eyes and scored a direct hit on the prosecutor. I glanced back to see whether the potential jurors had caught the display directed at Finn. Couldn't tell.

The judge kept her eyes on Finn for a few more seconds then moved them over to me. "Mr. Goodlove, do you wish to use one of your peremptory challenges?"

"I do not." *Win some, lose some.*

On the way back from the bench I leaned toward Finn and whispered, "Snake pit of pigs?"

She bumped me with her butt. *Intentional?*

I gave Jen the bad news. She absorbed it without a hint of emotion. Never let the jurors think you're losing. Carly also did a good job of hiding her thoughts.

Things started looking up as Finn blew through her own peremptory challenges. She apparently hadn't gotten the memo that striking jurors based on demographics was a waste of time.

For example, she was apparently trying to seat more males, and in the process seated Juror 7, a professor at HSU. We'd learned that he was known for his love of debating. He had an intellect tailor-made for the arguments we'd planned, and we predicted he would reject the gut-based anger that Finn was likely to try to evoke. Jen and I found it hard not to high-five when Finn let him onto the jury.

When we were done, however, the battle had gone to Finn in a big way. She'd been dealt a good hand, and she played it with a skill and flare that could have been used in a law school seminar. I could picture a professor tapping the screen with a pointer. "Now *that's* the way to win at jury selection."

We put on a good face for the public, but back at the office, Jen patted me on the shoulder. "It wasn't so bad."

"I keep picturing that big woman crossing her arms and shaking her head during deliberations."

"Dawson?"

"Yeah." I dropped into my chair, my head down.

"Chin up, boss. We don't have any indication that she's stubborn. Bigoted, a champion of the police, yes, but stubborn, no. You're too close to this. Step back and you'll see the big picture. Our professor will tie her up in knots. A hundred bucks says he'll be the foreman."

"Uh … no. No bet. I think you're right. I hope you're right."

I caught her looking at me with a worried frown. *Worry about the case, or worry about me?*

Louella was finishing up the report that would warm Garrett's heart: There was reasonable doubt as to who killed Angelo. More than reasonable. The mob was after him. Garrett would have to find a way to present that. Perhaps a judge could force the FBI to release enough information to get the charges dismissed.

That was not all. She'd uncovered a dirty trick the prosecution had up its sleeve. They probably wouldn't dare pull the trigger and call that witness. But if they did, Louella had information that would allow Garrett to keep her off the stand.

Just a few more sentences, then she'd send it. She was tired in a way only a heavy smoker can be, but she would sleep better once it was sent.

She coughed then froze. *Was there a noise behind that cough?* She pushed the button on her security system that turned on all the outside lights and paged between the different cameras. The rear corner camera was out again. Probably the same loose wire, but she couldn't take the chance.

After one last drag, she stubbed out her smoke and slid her laptop into its special slot. She took the shoulder holster off her desk. After putting it on over her housedress, she pulled out her pistol. It was a Smith and Wesson model 41. She gave it a quick once-over. She loved it; it hadn't jammed even once in the last year of target practice. She paged through the camera views again. *If I hadn't coughed, I'd know where the sound came from.*

Quail often tried to commit suicide by flying into her windows but not at night. They'd be roosting safely in the pine tree.

The guest room had a bay window with a clear view of the corner with the broken camera. She entered it, gun first, checked that it was clear, then closed the door so the room would be totally dark. Holding the gun down by her side, she eased onto the cushion below the window. It was a warm place to read when the sun was out.

She looked. Nothing happening at that corner of the house. Probably a false alarm.

Back in her office, she picked up the phone to dial 911 and report a possible prowler. Two things happened at once: The sound of shattering glass broke the silence, and the lack of a dial tone registered in her brain.

Showtime. Fuckers don't come into my *house.*

She had two options. She'd converted her office closet into a safe room, with a reinforced door and a solid lock. And a phone. A useless phone. That was out. If this was the mob Tick had talked about, they could get through the door or just burn down the house. Second option. Hunt the hunters or at least get to the cell phone in the front hall. She headed down the stairs, leading with her gun. The slightest movement from the corner at the bottom of the stairs and she'd shoot.

She got to the bottom and came around the corner. Again, the gun did the leading.

The living room was lit only by the streetlight down the block, and the phone sat in its charging dock in the hallway. *Screw it. I'm outta here. Elvis is in the building, and I'm too old to play cowboy. Slip out the door, and I can disappear into the neighborhood. As long as I don't have to run.*

She mentally rehearsed her moves: holster the gun, unlock the dead bolt, open the door, pull out the gun, go. She'd executed the first move, when a shadow flew out from the kitchen.

Her decades' old training kicked in. She pulled the gun from its holster and put a quick double tap in the guy's center of mass. No real thought; she just did it. He went down as if sliding headfirst into second base. His gun fell out in front of him, slid along the hardwood floor, and clattered into the bottom of the front door.

Breathing hard and trying to ignore the tightness in her chest, she kept her revolver trained on his head.

Guess there's some cowboy left in the old broad after all. The bad guy was all in black, with a dark balaclava on his head. She'd let the police roll him over. The risk wasn't worth going near him, even though he was probably dead.

Keeping the gun pointed at the perp, she picked up the cell phone. She was dying for another cigarette, but that could wait until the police were on their way.

Her attention divided between the dead guy and the phone, she didn't see the second intruder until he was halfway across the living room floor. *Damn!*

Her ottoman obsession saved her. She had four in the room, three more than any reasonable person would expect. The man tumbled over one, and his gun went off. The report was quiet. *A suppressor!*

She swung her gun over and pulled the trigger twice. Nothing. Jammed.

The man started to get up. Did he still have his gun in his hand?

No time to clear the jam. Three steps, and she was through the door into the basement. She locked it behind her. She'd had the lock put in for just this kind of situation, no matter how unlikely. Kind of a second safe room. She snapped on the light and ran down the stairs, her arthritic knees complaining with each impact.

Few houses in the neighborhood had full basements. Hers had a dirt floor and no door to the outside. *Fix the damn gun or climb out the window?* The bad guy was already attacking the door.

The window.

Pulling in wheezing breaths, she holstered the gun and cleared off the workbench below the window with one sweep of her arm. A paint can, a hibachi, and the toaster oven that her husband had never fixed crashed to the floor. Climbing onto the table, a pain gripped her chest as if someone were tightening a pipe clamp around it. *I am too old for this.*

She tried to unlatch the awning window, but it was rusted shut. She pulled out the gun and hit the lever. It came unstuck at the same time the basement door crashed open.

With the strength and speed provided by her sixty-five-year-old muscles, she pulled herself up and through the window. She stood in the recess, but before she could step up the two feet to ground level, a stinging sensation flashed up from her calf. *Gunshot?*

A second pain like the sting of a Doberman-sized wasp hit her. This time, she heard the pop of the gun. *You can hide, but you cannot run* went through her mind. She didn't have much time; the bad guy would be out the window soon. She felt sick—would it affect her thinking? *Where to hide?*

One time when her grandkids had played hide-and-seek in the yard, ten-year-old Melissa had discovered the best hiding place: A bear had hollowed out a den under a neighbor's shed, and bushes obscured the opening. Louella hobbled to it and crept in. *Unoccupied?*

No way the bad guy can find me here. But her relief called attention to her greater danger. The pain in her chest felt as if the den's former occupant were giving her a hug. She slid her hand to her calf. She probed the wounds. They felt like cuts from glass rather than bullet holes. It may have been the pain, the blood loss, or the probable heart attack—not that it mattered—one of those things or all of them together pushed Louella's mind toward the precipice of unconsciousness.

She had two final thoughts: No one would find her in time to save her, and she'd never see her grandkids again.

Chapter Fourteen

IN THE OLD DAYS, when I was a cutthroat, take-no-prisoners attorney, I'd have stayed up all night fine-tuning the next day's opening statement. However, after being schooled in the college of hard knocks on how depression and sleep deprivation were bosom buddies, I took no chances. I told myself I was ready to go and tucked myself into bed at 10:00 p.m.

I was sound asleep when my cell phone yanked me out of my dreams. I blinked at the bedside clock. 2:30 a.m. I hadn't dared set my phone to Do Not Disturb in case any last-minute emergencies needed my attention.

"Is this Mr. Garrett Goodlove?"

"Hold on a second." I took some deep breaths and rubbed my face. "Okay, sorry, go ahead … uh, yes, this is Mr. Goodlove."

"This is Police Chief Curtis in Weaverville. Do you have a son named Toby?"

"Yes. Is something wrong?" *Dumb question.*

Curtis had a southern accent. "We have Toby in custody here—"

"What is he charged with?"

"Now hold on, Mr. Goodlove. I'm on your side here. We haven't charged him with anything. He seems to be having some kind of episode or something. Does he have a mental condition?"

"What did he do?"

"Earlier this evening he was going from house to house, knocking on doors, and being really ... chatty. Nothing violent, but he really wanted to talk and was pretty insistent that people talk with him. We started getting phone calls. When we finally found him, he had climbed a tree and was yelling obscenities at people. We convinced him to come down, and we've brought him into the station. He's in a cell now."

"May I talk with him?"

"Yes, but first, can you tell me if y'all can come pick him up? We're pretty informal here, and I can release him to you. Can you do that?"

I looked at the clock. Three hours to Weaverville. "Do you have a hospital there?"

Curtis laughed. "No, I wouldn't call it that. It's just an emergency clinic. I'd have taken him there, but they're not equipped to handle anything like this. I've got a call in to a psychiatrist nearby, but I ain't been able to get a hold of her yet."

I did the math. Three hours there, three back. Admit him to St. Joe's? Could I find someone to babysit him? Leave him with a friend? Could I get to court in time?

"Okay," I said. "I'll leave immediately."

"That would be really good, sir. I get the feeling he's a good kid, but there's some kind of a screw loose in his head. I'm not a doctor, but this is serious, I think. We're in the Weaverville Town Hall, on the main drag. Just ring the buzzer. I'm going to hand the phone to him now."

Toby's voice faded in, as if he'd started talking before he had the phone up to his mouth. "Hey, Dad, do you know what's going on?"

"Toby, it—"

"I'm not sure how to get home from here. From Weaverville. That's where I am. They have me in jail here, and it's like Andy of Mayberry or something. Real small. But it really sucks. I don't know where my camera is. I've got a great idea for a photo book."

I once saw someone on TV who had won a prize for fast talking. Toby was faster.

"Toby, stop. Listen for a second. I'm going to come pick you up now. I want you to try to calm down and just wait for me. Do everything they tell you to. It will be okay."

Curtis came back on the line. "I'm not sure he got all that. He's pacing around now. I will see y'all soon. Drive careful."

I threw on some clothes and took two caffeine pills; I didn't want to take the time to make coffee. I was on the road in ten minutes, feeling a little manic myself. I gave my unconscious time to process things, then I started planning.

It sounded like I'd need to get Toby admitted to St. Joe's in Redwood Point. Carly was the best person to handle things there. She was smart, assertive, and levelheaded. On the other hand, she was going on trial for murder in just a few hours. If she went to the hospital, she'd be able to communicate with them, get things set up. I couldn't call Carly, but I could stop the car and text her.

Jen? No, I didn't want to wake her up. Someone had to be sharp for the trial. We'd gone over my opening statement together, maybe she could give it. *Would Judge Stevens let things start without my presence?*

I reached the windy part of Highway 299, and a tsunami of irrational and irresistible hopelessness washed over me. A twitch of the steering wheel, and I could drive off a cliff. It would be an accident. No one would know I abandoned them. *Stop! This is depression talking. You know better than to listen.*

Who else could I call? Louella. She'd gripe if I woke her up, but she'd want to help. Maybe she was awake. I set up the hands-free mode and dialed her number. *C'mon pick up.* It didn't go straight to voicemail, so her phone wasn't on Do Not Disturb. No answer. I left a message.

Did I really have no good friends that I'd feel comfortable calling? *Huh.* I hadn't realized until then that I'd let all my friendships lapse during my depression.

Nicole. Of course. She was at Quinnipiac University Law School in Connecticut, so three hours ahead. Her roommate answered then got the phone to Nicole.

"Dad?" She was probably squinting at the clock radio by her bed.

"Hey, sweetheart. I need your help with an emergency."

Her fog of sleep dissipated faster than mine had. She said, "Okay, I'm ready."

I explained the situation.

"Wait. Doesn't the trial start today? Are you going to make it?"

I sighed. "I don't know. It's a mess."

"You okay?"

"Yeah, I'm fine. Considering."

"Okay. You take him to the emergency room at St. Joe's. I'll call them to tell them you'll be there at … uh … around eight?"

"Yeah, something like that."

"Okay," she said. "I'll give Aunt Carly some more time to sleep, then I'll text her and get her over to the hospital."

"I'm not sure that she … with the trial and all."

"No. She can handle it. You should know that. Give me an update when you've got Toby. I'll call Jen at eight and give her a heads-up."

Was that a tear tickling my cheek? I wiped it away. "Thanks, sweetheart."

"Dad, you don't sound like yourself."

"Well, duh. I'm driving on a windy highway in drizzle at three thirty in the morning. I have a trial in— no, I'm fine, sweetheart."

"Call me when you have Toby."

"Will do."

Weaverville was deserted when I arrived. I parked and found the night bell by the door to the town hall. Police Chief Curtis himself answered, shaking my hand. He actually did have an Andy of Mayberry vibe.

Toby was released with a minimum of paperwork. Thank goodness he didn't have his episode in San Francisco. Of course, in that case he'd probably already be receiving excellent psychiatric care at the UCSF hospital.

He was still talking a mile a minute as he put on his seat belt. I made a U-turn, and we were headed back to Redwood Point.

"You're just leaving Weaverville now?" Nicole asked when I called her.

"Hey, I've been driving as fast as I can!"

"No, Dad, I'm just estimating when you'll get to St. Joe's. I'm not criticizing. I'm going to tell them you'll arrive at eight forty-five."

"Thanks, sweetheart. Sorry I snapped at you."

I hung up, and Toby had a rare moment of silence. I looked over at him.

"You're depressed again, Dad. Are you taking your pills?"

"No, I've been taking them. I just haven't gotten enough sleep." *Thanks to you,* I didn't add. "Carly's trial starts today, and I've got to, *got to* be in court at nine a.m."

I hadn't taken my antidepressant/sleep aid. If I had, I'd probably be in a ditch somewhere. But it didn't work the way Toby thought. That is, it changed my brain chemistry over the course of weeks; it wasn't an instant happy pill.

"They're not going to convict Aunt Carly, are they? I know she didn't do it. Hey, you want to rehearse?" Toby asked. "If you want to rehearse your opening statement, I'll try to shut the hell up for a while and listen."

Couldn't hurt. I launched into it as I had fifteen times over the last few days. Somehow it seemed weaker, almost hopeless.

"That was great, Dad." My son, the legal analyst. "You'll kill 'em dead. They won't convict her."

We pulled over to a roadside espresso stand, and I ordered a double shot macchiato for me and a mint tea for Toby. Giving him caffeine would be like administering cocaine to a hummingbird.

Back on the road, I asked, "Do you want to talk about what happened?"

"Later. I want to hear more about the trial."

I described my narrative of what I thought happened and went through the list of witnesses in alphabetical order. Jen wasn't the only one with a good memory.

"That's a lot of witnesses."

"Well, we're not going to call all of them. We have to supply the prosecution with the names of everyone we plan to call to the stand. Part of what's called 'discovery.' It's a common trick to put on a bunch of extra names, we call them 'chaff witnesses,' to hide the important ones."

"Sounds a little underhanded."

I sighed. "Yeah, it is, but everyone does it." Louella had checked out all the witnesses, but I hadn't received her report yet. That wasn't like her. Also, she'd given us a list of witnesses she thought we should call, but without the report, some were a mystery. For example, one was a tour operator from Arizona. *What was that about?*

"You mentioned Bridget Dundon. You know she was having an affair with Uncle Angelo, right?"

I almost drove off the road, the tires vibrating like a quiz-show buzzer on the rumble strip. "What?"

"Yeah. I walked in on them when they were doing it at Uncle Angelo's. I always thought men had affairs with women who are really different from their wives. I guess that's not always true. I don't like Bridget. At all. And I hate Uncle Angelo. I hate him! He got what he deserved." There was an intensity in his voice I'd never heard before. He gave me a quick glance.

"You saw this when Carly and Angelo were still together?"

He shrugged. "I don't remember. I backed out, you know, and they never knew I saw them."

Toby rambled on about other things for a few miles and talked about the Weaverville events in a way that didn't really make sense.

"Hey, buddy," I said. "I'd like to get you into the hospital so they can help us figure out what's going on with you." I held my breath.

I thought he wasn't going to reply, then he said, "Yeah. Okay. That's probably a good idea."

We pulled up to the emergency entrance at 9:00 precisely, same time the trial was supposed to begin. Carly stood outside the doors. She waved then stepped in through the doors, signed to someone, and came out again. She opened Toby's door and gave him a hug.

"We're all set." She handed me a clipboard with some forms to sign. I did so.

A nurse came out with a wheelchair. I blinked. It was none other than Bridget Dundon. She took the clipboard and my son and waved us off.

We burst through the courtroom doors at 9:20 and directly into the gale-force winds coming from Judge Stormy Stevens.

"So nice you could join us," she said.

"We had a family emergency, Your Honor."

"That is what Ms. Shek told us. If I find out this is one of your tricks, Mr. Goodlove, you'll find yourself in jail."

"I understand, Your Honor. It won't happen again." I was glad the jury wasn't in the box to hear that exchange.

I sat and whispered to Jen, "Louella?"

She shook her head. That was another emergency. Louella had told me her report was coming, but that was the last we heard from her. She'd implied the report included information that might help us stop the prosecution in its tracks. *We need that report!*

Chapter Fifteen

IT WAS TIME FOR opening statements. This was our only opportunity to make a good first impression on the jury. The visitors' gallery was full. Someone nearby was wearing too much perfume.

Finn sat at the prosecution table with Detective Crawford behind her, and the two of them had a whispered conference. Crawford sent a subtle sneer our way; I wasn't sure he was even aware of it.

Finn stood and stepped to the lectern. *Did she give me a tiny wink?* She cleared her throat. "Circumstantial evidence, ladies and gentlemen of the jury, has gotten a bad rap on TV."

The prosecutor was especially fetching in a navy blue top that contrasted perfectly with her hair. The neckline plunged just enough to show some cleavage—not quite over the line. The jurors were noticeably captivated, both men and women.

"But in fact," she continued, "the law tells us that circumstantial evidence and direct evidence are equally valid, and furthermore, that a jury can convict a defendant *solely* on the basis of circumstantial evidence. Let me make sure you understand these two terms."

I watched the jury for reactions and saw a little frown and smirk on Juror 2. He didn't like being lectured to as if he were a kid. I made a note.

Finn continued, "Let's say you look out the window, and you see that it's raining. That's direct evidence. But let's say you're in a courtroom such as this one that has no windows, and you see someone come in with a dripping umbrella. That's circumstantial evidence. You didn't see the rain, but you could infer that it was raining. Maybe your friend said, 'Gee, it's really raining hard out there.' More circumstantial but reliable evidence that it was raining.

"Ms. Carly Romero," Finn pointed, "pushed her husband off a high cliff onto the rocks below. No one saw her do it, but we will present conclusive circumstantial evidence that will convince you, beyond any reasonable doubt, that she murdered her husband. We have a witness who saw Ms. Romero leaving Tepona Point, the site of the murder, along a narrow path to the parking lot. A path along a ridge so narrow, that Ms. Romero could not have come from anywhere other than the site of the murder. She couldn't have just happened to stroll by from somewhere else.

"Our first witness, a surfer who was out on the ocean, saw Mr. Romero fall from the cliff in a manner that tells us that he was pushed. He didn't jump. This was no suicide, as the defense might want you to believe."

Finn walked to the prosecution table and drank from a sports bottle, giving her words a chance to sink in. "But that's not all. We have a close friend of the defendant's who will testify that Carly was outraged at her husband because she had just found out he had been having a long-term affair."

A murmur rolled through the audience, and a few jurors raised their eyebrows.

"That affair, she learned, had been going on when she was pregnant with her daughter. It continued while she was nursing the child and raising her together with her husband, Mr. Romero. It even continued, she'd learned, after that daughter of hers died at the age of only eighteen months! In her understandable rage at her husband, our witness will testify that the defendant said these chilling words." Finn picked up her pad as if she wanted to get them just right. "Please excuse the language, but Carly Romero said, using sign language, 'I'm going to push him off a fucking cliff!'"

Without another word, Finn went to the prosecution table and sat. She kept her eyes down.

I had to admit it, she was good. Her outrage was all an act, of course, but she played it perfectly. As the old joke goes: *The most important thing you need as a trial lawyer is sincerity. Once you can fake that, you've got it made.*

Stevens looked my way. "Mr. Goodlove."

"May it please the Court, Your Honor, I'd like to ask for the briefest of recesses."

Her eyebrows dropped from their usual unusually high position. "You certainly may not."

"No more than five minutes, Your Honor."

Probably assuming I was nervous and needed a bathroom break, she assented. "No more than five minutes."

"Thank you, Your Honor." I was already rushing down the aisle, ignoring Jen's and Carly's puzzled frowns. Let everyone think I had a weak bladder.

I ran through the hall, expecting to hear a bailiff's shout to stop. I didn't think I could make it to the car and back in five minutes, but I'd deal with Stormy Stevens's wrath later. My errand was worth it.

But then I saw the very thing I was intending to get from my trunk. It was broken but would meet my needs. I snatched it up and charged into the men's room. All the sinks were occupied, so I dipped my prop into the water of a toilet. I bent over and reached in and splashed water onto my hair. What I wouldn't do to gain my sister's freedom.

Back down the hall, I raised the umbrella and pushed through the courtroom doors backwards. I shook it, splashing water on some of the spectators, hoping I wouldn't read about an outbreak of *E. Coli* on the news. Every eye in the courtroom was on me.

Judge Stevens boomed, "Mr. Goodlove! What in the world is going on?"

"Well, Your Honor, I needed to get a little fresh air. As you know, it's a beautiful day and the sun is shining. But wouldn't you know it? Just when I was taking a deep breath, the sprinklers turned on. Lucky for me, I found this umbrella." I shook some more water onto the industrial carpet.

Stevens slammed her gavel. "I will not tolerate these kinds of tricks. My courtroom is not a circus. I am fining you one thousand dollars, payable after we adjourn for the day. There will be no more demonstrations like this … this … stunt that you just put on."

"I'm sorry, Your Honor."

"Please proceed with your opening statement."

I'd expected her rage and the sanction, but every juror got the message. They might even have enjoyed the little bit of excitement. I had them on my side.

Jen dried off my hair with some tissues. I decided to make no apologies.

"Ladies and gentlemen, circumstantial evidence can lead you astray. The prosecutor stated that by seeing a wet umbrella you could infer that it was raining. But it is not raining, and yet my umbrella is wet. A problem with circumstantial evidence is that it can lead you to an incorrect conclusion. Maybe the umbrella was wet because a sprinkler came on, or maybe someone dropped it in the … bathtub." I considered saying "toilet" but that would have been a distraction.

I took a breath. "Ms. Finn says that an eyewitness puts my sister—yes, the defendant is my very own dear sister—at the scene of the crime, but we'll show that her testimony has another, more plausible explanation, just as the wet umbrella had an explanation other than rain. We'll show that when Mr. Romero fell off the cliff, there was no way to know whether he jumped intentionally. Or tripped. Maybe he was taking a selfie too close to the edge. We have no direct evidence to tell us what happened."

I stopped and looked across the faces of the jurors. "Let me tell you a story. Many years ago I was married to a lovely woman. She was killed in a car accident, may she rest in peace. Raquel was Mexican and had a Latin temper. I had a temper, too, back then. One day, we were in the middle of a fight, I don't even remember what it was about. At one point, she screamed in frustration, like this—*Aaah!*—and ran out of the house." My scream was a good one and made everyone jump, especially Judge Stevens. "Raquel ran across the yard, jumped into our new car, and squealed out of the driveway. Unfortunately, in the process, she backed over the mailbox and sideswiped our big oak tree before peeling off down the road.

"You know what I did then? I remember it as if it were yesterday. Standing there in the front yard, I raised up my fists, like this, and you know what I said? I said, 'I'm going to strangle her!'"

I let that phrase hang in the air then said, "Of course I didn't mean it. I'm sure most of you have said something like that. 'I'm going to kill him.' 'I'm going to knock his fool head off.' I didn't mean it, and neither did you. When Raquel came back, I didn't strangle her, of course, even though I was still angry about the car. And the mailbox. We made up, and … uh … had a very nice evening together." Too much information?

Leave it there? No.

"During our case, we'll show you that the prosecutor, as she admits, has zero direct evidence that Angelo was murdered at all, let alone that my sister, Carly Romero, killed him. They'll present a meager few pieces of circumstantial evidence, but by applying a little common sense, you'll come to the conclusion that my sister had nothing to do with Mr. Romero's tragic death."

We could guess at some of Finn's strategy from her witness list, but without Louella's report, there were some scary holes. *Aargh.* I was sure she'd start with the surfer—show that Angelo had gone off the cliff—followed by the crabber to show that he'd died, and the eyewitness that put Carly at the scene.

Finn stood. "Your Honor, the People call Mr. Zeke Kapkowski to the stand."

The surfer had cleaned up well. His beard was gone, and he wore a tweed blazer over a white turtleneck. He went through the same story he'd given during the preliminary hearing: A sound had made him look toward Tepona Point. He saw a man tumble off the cliff and into the ocean.

An airhorn had been found near the edge of the drop-off, and the police had collected it as evidence. Was that relevant? Could that be the noise the surfer had heard?

Finn had brought out the surfer's impression that the man had been pushed off the cliff. In fact, as often happens, the man's conclusions had solidified from *It kinda looked like he was pushed* to *He was definitely pushed.* That's the way the brain works. Perhaps his subconscious was eager to please the sexy prosecutor.

Finn sat, and it was my turn. I stood and walked to the lectern.

"Mr. Kapkowski, did Mr. Romero yell out, '*Aah!* Someone pushed me off the cliff!' when he fell?" Leading questions are allowed during cross, and I use them as often as possible. They allow me to keep some control over the answers.

Finn stood. "Objection."

The judge and I both looked at her. Stevens asked, "On what grounds?"

Finn frowned. "Uh … withdrawn." She sat back down.

Kapkowski turned to the judge.

She nodded. "You may answer."

"No. That's a stupid question," he said. "Of course I couldn't hear him. He was about three hundred meters away, and the swell was humongous. Loud."

"Mr. Kapkowski, please just answer Mr. Goodlove's questions."

"Yes, Your Honor. Sorry. No, I couldn't hear him."

"Did you see Mr. Romero shake his fist at anyone, like, 'I'm gonna *get* you for this'?"

A few spectators and two jurors laughed. Jurors are usually pretty bored. They'd rather be somewhere else, and their minds can wander. Putting on a little show helps them pay attention.

"No, he was too far away for me to see anything like that."

"And yet from that distance you could tell someone pushed him."

"Yes, it was the way that—"

"Thank you. Did you see anyone push him?"

"No. I only saw him fall, but—"

"Did you see my sister, Carly, push him?"

"No. I was out in the lineup, so I had to keep my eye on incoming swells."

"The lineup? Can you tell the jury what that refers to?"

He looked toward the jury box. "It's the place where the waves break. It's where the surfers line up to catch them."

"Ah, I see. And the waves were big that day?"

"Yeah. Double overhead." He glanced at the jurors. "They were twice as tall as I am."

"And I guess, if you're not paying attention, they can really clobber you, is that right? You had to keep an eye out?"

"Objection as to form."

"Sustained."

Finn was just trying to break my rhythm.

"Sorry. You could really get clobbered if you weren't paying attention. Isn't that right?"

"Yes."

"So, at this great distance, and with your attention divided between the waves and this falling body, it seemed to you that the body had been pushed?"

"Yes. Definitely."

I was tempted to ask why but didn't. A famous lawyer, R. Eugene Pincham, once joked, "I asked a witness 'why' on cross-examination twenty years ago. When I stopped by that courtroom a few days ago on my way here, the witness was still on the stand answering that question."

"Was it because the man was tumbling through the air?"

"It wasn't no cliff dive, like in Acapulco."

I froze. Something about that seemed important, but I didn't know why.

Judge Stevens asked, "Mr. Goodlove?"

"Sorry. The man's body was tumbling, is that right?"

"Yes, I just said that."

"You've seen Tepona Point up close. Is that right?"

"Yes. When the waves were smaller, I paddled close to it."

"Is it a straight shot from the tip of the cliff to the ocean below?"

"No, there are some parts, some rocks, that stick out."

"Have you walked out on Tepona Point?"

"Yeah."

"Can you see those outcroppings from the edge?"

He shook his head. "Not really."

"Yes or no, please, Mr. Kapkowski. Can you see them or not?"

"No."

"Permission to approach the witness, Your Honor?"

Stevens said, "Uh, yes."

I stepped away from the lectern. "What would happen if I fell like this?" I summoned all of my acting skills, and, drawing from personal experience, put a look of intense depression on my face. On two occasions, I'd stood on the span of a high bridge but lacked the energy to climb over the railing and jump. Many depression sufferers are saved from themselves only because they don't have enough spirit to commit suicide. To act. Trying to convey all of that, I hung my head and arms and let myself fall forward. I'd intended to catch myself at the last second but failed, and I dropped to the courtroom floor on my hands and knees. I stood back up. "What would have happened if I'd fallen off the cliff like that?"

"You would have hit the, uh, outcroppings."

"Excuse me, could you speak up?"

"You would have hit the outcroppings," he said, "and then tumbled."

"And then tumbled," I repeated. "So, if a depressed person, someone too tired to go on living, wanted to commit suicide, might he wait for a day with double-overhead waves then simply let himself fall from the cliff?"

"Objection. Calls for speculation."

"Sustained."

"No further questions, Your Honor."

"Redirect, Ms. Finn?"

"No, Your Honor." She, along with the jurors, had heard the surfer's tone change from certainty to doubt, and it was unlikely she could reverse that.

The court recessed for lunch, and Jen, Carly, and I drove to my office to confer in private. We'd learned the hard way that ASL conversations were only private when surrounded by four walls. A pizza was waiting for us on the floor outside the office door; Jen had arranged to have it delivered.

I called the hospital and was told that Toby was doing fine in the locked psych ward. They wouldn't let me talk with him but told me to expect a progress report in a day or so.

I texted Nicole, thanking her for her excellent work and giving her the latest news.

Jen told me I'd "done good." In between bites of pizza, I translated our conversation into ASL.

She asked, "How did you get the umbrella so fast? You didn't plan that ahead of time, did you?"

"Dumb luck. I found it in the hall. Discarded. I was going to get mine from the car, but the delay probably would have pushed Stormy Stevens over the edge. I had planned to talk about the pitfalls of circumstantial evidence, and when Finn used the umbrella example, I knew what I had to do."

"Ah. And you splashed water on it and on your head from the water fountain."

"Not exactly."

Carly frowned. Jen cocked her head.

"You don't want to know."

Jen was a bit of a germaphobe. Carly signed, "Tell us."

"The toilet in the men's restroom."

Carly laughed, and Jen put her slice of pizza in the trash and went to wash her hands.

When she was back, Carly said, "Angelo wasn't depressed."

"You were separated, so how would you know?"

"Angelo was never depressed."

I shrugged. "It doesn't matter. Even if Finn can elicit testimony that suggests Angelo would never off himself, I can knock it down. Anyone can get depressed. I have an expert ready to testify to that, but I don't think Finn wants to touch it."

Soon, the whole office smelling like a pizzeria, I turned to Carly. "Once again, you're sure it wasn't you that the eyewitness saw at Tepona?"

She clenched her jaw the way she often did. "Correct. I did not go out on the point. I was coming back from Clam Beach. Along the road."

"And you didn't see that woman? Ms. Dowzer."

"No."

"Okay." I took a breath. "Let's finish up and stop by Louella's. I'm getting a very bad feeling about her."

As expected, Louella wasn't home. I'd forgotten to bring the key she'd given me years ago. We banged and yelled, but no one came to the door. I looked in through the peephole but couldn't see anything.

I asked Jen. "What was the name of her partner at RPPD?"

"Vince Rolewicz."

I called RPPD and left a message for him, asking him to look into Louella's disappearance.

Chapter Sixteen

FINN ROSE. "THE PEOPLE call Ms. Yvette Dowzer."

Still looking fit and trim, she walked to the witness chair and sat. No stoop. She didn't move like the senior citizen that she was.

Ms. Dowzer's testimony about seeing Carly on the trail from Tepona Point matched what she'd said in the preliminary hearing. As with the surfer, time had made her more certain about what she'd seen. Finn went through the testimony with no surprises.

My turn. "Ms. Dowzer, you testified that the woman you saw was wearing a Bizet University hoodie, is that right?"

"Yes."

"Are those sweatshirts pretty common around here?"

"Yeah, I guess so. There are a lot of deaf students in this area."

"Thank you." I produced a portion of the transcript from the preliminary hearing and introduced it into evidence. "May I approach the witness, Your Honor?"

Stevens assented, and I handed the sheet of paper to the witness. "Ms. Dowzer, this is a transcript of your prior testimony. Could I ask you to read the highlighted text on this sheet? Out loud?"

She put on her reading glasses. "Let's see. 'Q' means 'question'?"

"That's right."

"Okay. 'Question: Ms. Dowzer, can you tell us anything more about what you saw? Answer: Well, I do admit that I only got a very quick look at her face. Just a flash, you know. I guess I kinda felt that the woman was —'"

"That's enough. Thank you. You only saw her face very briefly. Now I'd like to call your attention to the next exhibit." I went through the process of having it entered. "Is this the photo Detective Crawford showed you when he came to your house?"

"Yes, I think so."

"Do you think it's possible that seeing this photo all by itself may have seared the image of Carly Romero into your mind and kind of cemented that brief flash of a face into your memory so that later, when you saw multiple pictures, you picked that one as the face of the woman you saw?" I was going into dangerous territory, but I was depending on the witness's qualifications of her answers in the past. This woman didn't feel she could rely on her memory. One of her Facebook posts had indicated she thought maybe she was getting Alzheimer's.

She shook her head. "No, I don't think that happened. I remember the face."

Darn. I'd printed out her Facebook post, made a year earlier. I entered that as the next exhibit then handed it to her. "Can you read the highlighted Facebook post out loud, please?"

"Uh … it says, 'I'm not remembering things as well as I used to. Alzheimer's?'"

"Do you remember posting that?"

"Yes. Yes, I do." The uncertainty on her face was a blessing. *Did the jury notice?*

"You are under oath here, Ms. Dowzer, and your answer is very important. Do you want to reconsider what you said about remembering the face?"

She looked at the photo again then frowned and pulled on her ear. "Yes, I guess that's possible, if I understood your question. Yeah, I could have seen this photo and then remembered it later."

Phew.

"But I don't think that's what happened."

I got the next exhibit entered, a stiff card printed with an array of photos—known as a "six-pack"—used when Ms. Dowzer identified Carly down at the station. Judge Stevens frowned deeply when she saw it and sent a scowl toward the prosecution table. Her ire was undoubtedly directed at Crawford.

I handed it to the witness. "Do you remember when Detective Crawford gave you this sheet and asked you to pick out the photo of the woman you saw at Tepona Point?"

She gave a tiny laugh. "Yes."

"Can you tell us why you're laughing?"

"Yes," she said. "I remember laughing when I saw these the first time, because one of the pictures was a black lady."

"And why was that funny?"

"Well, there aren't many black people in this area, and if the woman I'd seen was black, I would have mentioned that to the detective, so it seemed funny for him to have put a black lady in the pictures."

"Do you think the detective did that because he wanted you to choose the photo of my sister?"

Finn jumped up so fast her feet might have left the ground. "Objection! Your Honor, please!"

"I withdraw the question. No further questions."

Judge Stevens said, "Redirect, Ms. Finn?"

Finn took no time to get to the lectern. "Mr. Goodlove seemed to imply the detective may have tried to influence your identification of the defendant. Was your identification influenced?"

"Well," she said, "It could have been … but, no, I know who I saw."

"And who was that?"

"The woman. Ms. Romero." She pointed to Carly.

"May the record show that Ms. Dowzer pointed to the defendant." By always referring to Carly as "the defendant," Finn hoped to dehumanize her. "And you're absolutely positive of that, beyond any doubt. Is that so?"

I could have objected on the grounds that the question had already been asked and answered, but I didn't want to bring any more attention to it.

Dowzer said yes.

"No further questions." Finn looked over her notes.

Her next witness was Wenzel Rozetti, the amateur crabber who had seen Angelo's body in the ocean but failed to retrieve it. Like the surfer, the crabber cleaned up well: a good pair of slacks, a blue shirt, and a darker blue tie. He held the tie's knot, lifted his chin, and rotated his head back and forth. He was either unaccustomed to wearing a tie, nervous about speaking in public, or both.

Finn led him through his testimony about discovering the body and getting some of its DNA on his boat hook. Angelo had died, and his body had washed out to sea. That wasn't a big blow to our case.

Louella had researched him, but we hadn't gotten her report. *Where are you, Louella?*

When Finn was finished with her direct, Judge Stevens turned to me. "Mr. Goodlove?"

"I have no questions, Your Honor, but I would ask the Court to ensure that Mr. Rozetti remains available for later questioning and that he be excluded from the courtroom until that time." Louella had put him on our witness list.

We were packing up our materials when Jen squeezed my arm. Hard. *Ow.* She showed me the text on her phone.

Louella Davis is at St. Joseph Hospital.

Well, that explained why we hadn't heard from Louella. I should have figured it out. I guess I must have known she was in some kind of trouble, but with the start of the trial and my son's mental breakdown, my brain pushed that information to the back burner. If my inaction resulted in her death, I'd never forgive myself.

Louella was in a coma in the ICU, her daughter, Gail, by her bedside. The docs didn't want me in there, but Gail insisted. Jen waited in the hall.

Louella didn't look good. I leaned down to her. "I'm here, Louella. We're all pulling for you." I wiped some tears away with my thumb and forefinger and stood to give Gail a hug. Gail was a tough broad, like her mom. She even looked like a younger version of Louella.

Gail spoke in low tones. "They found her yesterday underneath a shed in a neighbor's yard. She was wearing a housecoat, and she had her shoulder holster over it. With her gun."

"What? Really?"

She ignored my question. "They wouldn't have found her except that someone was walking their dog, and he was barking and sniffing at the shed. She had embedded glass and cuts on her calf. She lost a lot of blood."

"Oh, jeez. What do the doctors say?"

"They give her a fifty-fifty chance of coming out of the coma, but even if she does, she might be bedridden the rest of her life. She had a heart attack. The police went to her house and found a dead body."

"What?" I paced around in a circle. Was this related to her investigation into Angelo's background? *Must be.* What had she said? DialUSA was sketchy, and someone had warned her to mind her own business.

Would Judge Stevens call a mistrial if this was related? Possibly. Did I want that? Too early to tell.

I hugged Gail again and whispered to Louella that I'd be back—*could she hear me?*—then collected Jen and drove to Louella's house. Squad car flashers bounced off the sides of the houses and made the fog glow. The police were investigating and wouldn't let us in. Her former partner Vince Rolewicz met us at the crime scene tape.

"They were pros, but that's about all we know."

I wanted to tell him about DialUSA and Louella's suspicions, but that could wait. *Hold on.* "You need to put a guard on her at the hospital. Someone might still want her dead."

He blinked. "There wasn't a guard? I'll take care of it." He started toward the house.

I called him back. "Detective Rolewicz, there's information on her laptop that's protected by attorney-client privilege. If you find—"

"We haven't found a laptop. There's none here." He went back into the house.

That puzzled me for a few seconds, then I nodded. I knew why they hadn't found it.

The next morning, Finn called Bridget Dundon to the stand. We'd been able to exclude the video of the damaging ASL conversation, but that didn't mean the conversation was out-of-bounds. Both Finn and I had the precise transcript of what was said, but if she referred to it, the judge would call a mistrial. Still, knowing exactly what was said could guide Finn's questioning.

Bridget seemed extremely reluctant to testify against her supposed best friend. Of course, Carly didn't know it was Bridget who'd had the long-standing affair—according to Toby, at least—with Angelo.

Stupid, stupid, stupid. I should have prepared Carly for that revelation, just in case. In my defense, I had a lot going on. If that came out in testimony, Carly would go ballistic. In front of the jury.

But Finn doesn't know. I relaxed, but just in case, I wrote, *No matter what you hear, keep your cool. Show no reaction. Very important.* I underlined "important" three times.

Carly and Jen both frowned at me. Like: *What the hell is that all about?*

I mouthed, "Okay?" to Carly, and she nodded.

Finn glanced at my legal pad on her way to the lectern, but I covered my writing with my hand.

"Ms. Dundon," she said, "do you remember a conversation you had with the defendant toward the end of November of last year?"

Bridget looked at Carly and rubbed her fist on her chest in a tiny circle, the sign for "sorry." She did it so unobtrusively that perhaps no one else noticed. Judge Stevens would have had a conniption if she'd seen it or saw Carly respond. I wrote, *Hands in your lap* on my pad.

The translator put Finn's question into sign. Bridget answered, "Yes," and the translator spoke the word.

"Can you tell us what the conversation was about?"

"A woman had sent an anonymous email to Carly telling her that someone had been having an affair with her husband. For years. Carly was very angry and was venting her frustration to me." Bridget was sweating and not simply because the court's heating system was cooking us alive. What stress she must have been under, talking about her own betrayal and hoping Carly wouldn't figure things out. I shook my head. *What a shit this woman is.*

I followed along as Bridget related the conversation. Finn had probably given her a transcript of the video to refresh her memory. Bridget followed the script pretty well.

"Can you tell us what she said at the end of the conversation?"

"She just said goodbye."

Finn pushed a lock of her orange-red hair behind an ear. "I'm sorry. I meant before she said goodbye."

Bridget breathed deeply.

"Ms. Dundon?"

"She said, 'I'm going to push him off a fucking cliff.'"

The translator hesitated and then translated, using the word "fucking" instead of something like "expletive."

The gasps from the spectators, and the jurors, hit me like a punch to the gut. It was the reaction I'd feared, only worse. I didn't let on, and neither did Jen. There's a saying: The best trial lawyers are never caught off guard even when they're caught off guard. Never let them see you sweat.

Carly did a good job of hiding her emotions as well, although at close range her jaw muscle twitches were clear to me.

Finn nodded. "I'm going to repeat that so we can be sure that the translator—"

"Objection!" This time I was the one popping to my feet like a jack-in-the-box. "Asked and answered. The translator did fine. There is no need to repeat anything."

"Sustained."

Finn spent more time on it, trying to milk it for everything it was worth. It was a mistake. I would have sat down, allowing the phrase to sit in the minds of the jurors for as long as possible. Time and again, when jurors fill out questionnaires, one of the top complaints is that lawyers repeat themselves trying to hammer their points home. *We got it the first time!* they write.

Finally, Finn sat down.

My turn. "Ms. Dundon, when Carly said that, did you think she was serious? That she really wanted to kill her husband?"

"Objection! Calls for speculation."

"Okay. Have you ever been mad at someone and said something that you didn't mean? Like 'I'm gonna strangle him'?"

Bridget knew where I was going and was happy to help. "Yes. Many times."

"But you didn't really want to strangle anyone, did you?"

"No. Not at all."

"It was just a figure of speech, wasn't it?"

"Yes. Absolutely."

"Did you call the police when Carly said that?"

She frowned, genuinely puzzled. "No. Of course not."

"Is that because you knew Carly didn't really want to kill her husband?" I asked.

"Objection. Calls for speculation."

"Not at all, Your Honor. I'm not asking Ms. Dundon to speculate about what *Carly* was thinking. I'm just asking about her own state of mind. Why she didn't call the police."

"I'll allow it. Overruled."

It was a little confusing with the translation going back and forth. Bridget said, "What was the question?"

"I asked why you didn't call the police. Was it because you knew Carly didn't really want to kill her husband?"

"Yes. Yes, exactly."

"You knew that what she said was just a figure of speech. She didn't mean it."

"Objection as to form. Compound question."

"Sustained."

Fine with me. I got to drive home the point some more. "You knew that what she said was just a figure of speech."

"Yes."

"You knew that she didn't really mean it."

"Yes, yes! I knew she didn't mean it."

"No further questions, Your Honor." *That* was the way to leave your important point in the jurors' minds. I had to resist the impulse to high-five with Jen. I saw the admiration in her eyes. *Way to go, boss!*

I glanced over at Finn. Nothing like kicking a little ass to relieve depression.

Not little. A nicely sized ass.

Chapter Seventeen

THE HEATING SYSTEM WAS still in overachiever mode, and I guessed the temperature in the courtroom was getting up toward the eighties. With the court staff, jurors, and spectators all sweating, it felt as if we were holding the trial in a locker room.

"Can't they just switch it off?" Jen asked.

I shrugged. "This is the government."

Finn stood. "The People call Ms. Jackie Rice to the stand."

Ms. Rice had one of the strangest hairstyles I've seen. It was helmet hair, but not in the sense of being treated with so much hairspray that it could protect your head in case of a fall. Her hair resembled a black motorcycle helmet, with straight-across bangs and sides that came down and hugged the lines of her jaw. If she'd lifted it off and placed it on the railing, it wouldn't have surprised me.

Finn ran through Ms. Rice's background, probably expecting me to stipulate as to her experience. I kept my eyes on my pad. Finn tended to bore the jury, and I wasn't going to help her speed things up. Next, she had the witness explain how modern computer browsers maintain a history of sites visited and searches made. She introduced People's Exhibit 1, a printout of Carly's browser history and Exhibit 2, a list of the files in the documents folder.

"Can you tell us, Ms. Rice, what struck you when you went through the browsing history?"

"Well, yes. She was obviously looking for ways to murder her—"

I stood. "Move to strike."

The judge turned to the witness. "Ms. Rice, please report only what you saw and not any conclusions you reached. Is that clear?" She then instructed the jury to ignore the witness's response.

Finn repeated the question.

"Well, she was—there were a lot of searches concerning how to kill someone. And how to get away with it."

"I've highlighted some of those searches in yellow. Could you read them out to the court?"

"Yes, I can. Let's see ... 'Best way to kill someone,' 'How to get away with murder,' 'Can you poison someone with a transdermal patch?' 'Undetectable poisons.'" Rice read about six more before Finn stopped her.

"Would those types of searches be consistent with someone who wanted to—"

"Objection. Leading. Calls for speculation."

"Sustained. Ms. Finn, you've been warned."

She'd made her point and continued to guide the witness through the different searches Carly'd performed and the websites she'd visited. Did she not notice the fidgeting going on in the jury box?

Finally, Finn sat.

I stood and moved to the lectern. "Ms. Rice, did you find any searches for how to push someone off a cliff?"

"No."

"Anything on how far someone had to fall to die?"

"No, but maybe she—"

"Thank you. How about any research on the heights of cliffs along the Pacific? Tepona Point, for example?"

"Objection. Compound question."

I looked at Finn. *Really?*

"Sustained."

It wasn't really worth objecting to, but it disrupted my rhythm. I asked the two questions separately and got a negative answer for each.

"Ms. Rice, what did you think of how Ms. Romero organized her computer?"

"Excuse me?"

"You're an expert on computers. You've seen the information on a lot of computers. Was Carly Romero's well organized?"

"Objection as to relevance. Where is this going?"

"Your Honor, the relevance will become apparent very soon."

"I'll allow it," Stevens said.

"It was very well organized. The files were where they should be, the desktop was neat, the Gmail in-box wasn't stuffed with emails like I see with most people's computers."

"We've heard testimony that Ms. Romero graduated at the top of her class in college, would you say that her intelligence level is reflected in the organization of her computer?"

Finn stood again. "Your Honor, please. What possible relevance—"

"Let's get to the point, Mr. Goodlove."

"I will, Your Honor."

"Yes," Rice said, "I had the impression Ms. Romero was a smart person."

"Thank you. Referring to People's Exhibit 1, could you turn to page twelve?"

She picked up the sheaf of papers and paged through them.

"Please read the second line on that page."

"Uh ... it says, 'If you kill someone, don't Google how to do it first.'"

The sigh of frustration that came from behind me suggested that Finn had just figured out where I was going.

I said, "That's the title of a web page Ms. Romero visited, is that right?"

"Yes."

"Can you tell me how long she spent on that website?"

"It was visible for eight minutes, although of course I can't say how long she looked at it."

"Fair enough. At this time, I'd like to introduce Defense Exhibit 1." I took three copies of the printout and handed one each to Finn, the judge, and the witness. "Can you please read the title of the web page for the court?"

Rice cleared her throat. "'If you kill someone, don't Google how to do it first.'"

"Thank you. Could you read the text I've highlighted?"

"'The defendant Googled "chemicals to passout a person," "make someone pass out," "how to suffocate someone," "most reliable poisons," and over fifty other searches related to murder. At trial, the defendant's search history was used to not only convict her but also show that the murder was premeditated.'"

"Thank you. To be clear, this is a website talking about someone else's trial. So when it talks about 'the defendant,' it's talking about the defendant in that trial, does that sound right?"

"Yes."

"And in that trial, someone was convicted based on his Google searches. Is that how you understand it?"

"Yes."

"Me, too," I said. "Now, you've testified that Ms. Romero seemed smart and that she knew her way around a computer. If she were using her computer to search for ways to kill someone and she read that article, wouldn't she delete her browsing history?"

"If she knew how to do it."

"It's pretty simple isn't it?"

Rice looked at the prosecution table. "I guess it is."

"Even if Ms. Romero didn't know how to do it, she was probably smart enough to find out how."

"Yes."

"Could you speak up please?"

"Yes. But why else would she be researching methods of killing someone?"

I laughed. "That's a good question. An excellent question. Let's see if we can answer that, shall we?"

God, I was having fun. Walking to the exhibit cart, I picked up People's Exhibit 2, the list of Carly's files, and asked to approach the witness. I gave it to her. "On page fifteen, tenth line down, could you read us the name of the file you see?"

"'SJ.docx'?"

"Yes, that's the one. Did you have a chance to examine that file?"

"Uh … not that I remember. Do you know how many files are on a computer?"

"Very many, I understand. It's not at all surprising that you couldn't examine them all. I have printed out the contents of that file, and I am introducing it as Defense Exhibit 2."

Finn stood. "Your Honor, this is the first we've heard of … never mind." She sat down again. She'd had the file in her possession, so she couldn't complain.

I handed out the copies. "Could you read the top two lines?"

"'Silent Justice. By Carly Goodlove Romero.'"

"Thank you. Please read the first four paragraphs out loud." Normally, I'd avoid having a witness read such a long selection, but this one would keep them entertained.

Rice started reading. This is how Carly's thriller began:

> Gary Goodson only had a few minutes to live.
> The long string of days extending back to the day he was born was about to come to an end.

His plans for the night included only getting very drunk and getting very laid. This was his third date with Kathy, and she'd shown all the signs of being ready to go to bed with him. *Hadn't she?* He probably should have been more insistent during their last date, but it didn't matter. Tonight was the night.

Following his shower, he pulled the box of "Party Time" transdermal patches from the bathroom cabinet and took out the last one. He didn't see the tiny hole in the foil casing, but he did notice that when he tore it open some liquid squirted onto the bathroom floor. That hadn't happened with the other ones. He shook his head. *So much for quality control.* He removed the backing that covered the patch's adhesive and applied the thing to his upper arm. *No hangover for me.* Googling told him the patches were just snake oil, but he didn't care. They worked for him. They weren't perfect, but his hangovers hadn't been as bad since he got the patches.

It was when he pulled up his pants that he first noticed the weakness. They seemed to weigh twenty pounds. All his clothes seemed heavy, in fact, and breathing seemed to take a conscious effort, as if someone had strapped a belt around his chest. While contemplating this, he collapsed to the floor, knocking his head on the corner of his dresser and landing in a heap. *What the hell is going on?*

"That's enough, thank you," I said. "What do you think that was?"

"It seems to be the start of a book. Or some kind of a story." The witness glanced at Finn.

Jen and I had read the first several chapters of the book. That's all Carly had written so far. After Gary Goodson died, we were introduced to the book's main character, an LA police detective who was strong, good looking, and deaf. She was called to the crime scene and made sure the techs collected the small spot of yellow goo on the bathroom floor.

"You think the name is significant?" Jen had asked me.

"What do you mean?"

"Gary Goodson, Garrett Goodlove. I zink maybe vee have here some unconscious hostility, ya?"

I'd smiled. "Maybe, Sigmund."

In court, I thanked Ms. Rice for her reading. She actually had a flair for drama and a pleasing voice. She could probably make a living narrating audiobooks. "Ms. Rice, what would you say is happening in the beginning of that scene, perhaps drawing on your expertise as a crime investigator?"

"It's obviously some kind of a thriller. It starts by saying a man only has a few minutes to live. Then he puts on some kind of transdermal patch, but it seems that someone has tampered with the patch. Then he collapses."

"Very good. Why do you think he collapsed?"

She had a *Duh!* expression on her face. Like *I'm a professional. Of course I get it.* "It's obvious that someone put some kind of poison in the patch that he put on his arm."

"Thank you. Now, can you reread line ... forty-seven in People's Exhibit 1?"

It took her a bit to find the relevant page. "Uh ... 'Can you poison someone with a transdermal patch?'"

"That was something Ms. Romero searched for?"

"Yes."

"Huh. I guess we know now why Carly was searching all those terms."

"Objection!"

"Sustained."

"No further questions."

Jen and I had argued about what to do with that evidence. Often, when you have some exculpatory information, the first impulse is to bring it to the attention of the DA's office, hoping they won't want to proceed with the case. That is, they'll dismiss the charges. However, that impulse can be misguided. The danger is that it will just tip them off to your strategy and give them an advantage at trial.

But Finn's team had the laptop, and we'd gambled they wouldn't look at the file containing her work in progress. They hadn't, giving us a chance to detonate an unsuspected improvised explosive device in the heart of their case.

Judge Stevens was melting, her thin, old-lady hair now wilted like waterlogged angel hair pasta. It was time for her to announce the lunch break. A man in blue coveralls bustled up the aisle and went straight to the bench. He whispered something to the judge then turned and left.

"Ladies and gentlemen," Stevens said, "due to a problem with the heating system, we will stand adjourned until tomorrow morning at nine." She cracked the gavel.

Another good break for our team. The jurors would have all night to think about how the prosecution had overreached, trying to make mountains out of what turned out to be molehills.

Once the prosecution rests, the defense usually makes a motion to dismiss the charges, arguing that the state has failed to prove its case. *If this is all they have, this nightmare could be over in a day or two.*

I started second-guessing my decision not to disclose the reason for the web searches earlier. Maybe they would have dropped the charges then. On the other hand, they might have gone ahead anyway, relying on the testimony from the eyewitness and Bridget Dundon. They would have avoided the day's crippling setback that made them look like incompetent clowns.

I expected dejected looks at the prosecution table, and Crawford indeed sat slouched, scowling at the floor. Finn, however, looked fresh as a shamrock and wore a Mona Lisa smile. She'd tied her hair up into a bun, less hot than having it insulate the back of her neck, I guessed. She caught me looking and gave a little flick of her head: Come and see me.

I nodded.

Carly wrote, *What does she want?*

I scribbled, *Probably wants a plea deal.*

"No!"

I signed back, "Okay."

I hung back after Carly, Jen, and most everyone else had left the courtroom then went over to Finn's table. She was standing, putting her papers in the briefcase.

She smiled. "How about dinner tonight?"

"We're not interested in a plea deal."

She looked around as if she'd heard voices and couldn't tell where they were coming from. "Did someone say, 'plea deal'? I sure didn't."

"Good. Let's keep it that way."

"So, how about dinner? My treat. And I promise there will be no pleas, at least none related to the case." She winked.

What the hell did that mean? "Are you about to wrap up your case?"

"Pretty soon."

"Yeah, I better take a rain check. For after the trial."

She shook her finger at me. "Garrett, didn't your mother tell you never to delay gratification?"

"Uh … no, actually." I laughed. "That's the opposite of something she might have said. I'm pretty sure no mothers say that."

She laid a heavy brogue on. "Gather ye rosebuds while ye may, old time is still a-flying; and this same flower that smiles today tomorrow will be dying."

"Carpe diem."

"Exactly. It's from the poem 'To the Virgins, to Make Much of Time.'"

"I'm confused. That would be relevant to you how?"

"Ha ha. Pick you up at six?"

I looked at my watch. "Better make it seven. I have some—"

"Rosebuds to gather."

"Exactly."

Back at the office, Jen did *not* like that I was going on a date with Finn.

"It's just dinner, not a date," I said.

"Oh, my mistake."

"Stop pacing. You're making my legs tired."

"Oh, we wouldn't want that. Wouldn't want you to have tired legs on your dinner date."

"Good point. I always like to do some power squats between courses. Jen, I've never seen you like this. What's going on?"

She sat down and gave me her trademark stare.

"That's better. Inscrutable I can understand. This pacing business—" I fluttered my hand "—it's like you're someone I don't know."

"Does Carly know you're going out with Finn?"

"Again, not a date really, and yes, she knows and approves."

"Approves?"

"Yes. She feels that if Finn falls in love with me, she's less likely to want to convict my sister."

"A little late for that, don't you think? And love? It's not a date, but she's falling in love with you?"

"Carly said that, not me. I don't think Finn's interested in me that way."

"Boss, you really are clueless. You haven't noticed that most women are interested in you that way?" She swept her arm as if to encompass the entire population of the planet.

"Including you?" I said it as a joke but was shocked when Jen blushed the color of Japanese cherry blossoms. Another new experience.

Jen stood up and went to her office, slamming my door on the way. Then her door.

Huh.

Down on the street, Finn honked the horn of her red—of course—Mazda Miata. She had the top up and the flashers on. It was 7:30. Finn was running on what we call "Humboldt time."

During the afternoon I'd gone over the witnesses on my list, putting them in the best order in case we got to that part of the trial. I called the hospital, but there was no change in Louella's condition. I confirmed that I was on the approved visitor list for her; her daughter had taken care of that. Jen had recovered from her uncharacteristic snit, and we'd discussed which witnesses she'd take.

I locked up and went down the stairs and out to the car. Was Jen right? Did this not-a-date have something to do with the case? Louella's words also echoed in my mind: *She's sneaky. I wouldn't trust her as far as I could throw her.* But perhaps I could get some information out of Finn that would help Carly. *I can be sneaky, too.*

The passenger door popped open when I got to the sidewalk. I stepped in, and she pulled out immediately.

"Sorry I'm late," she said. "I didn't want to seem like an eager beaver. How do you feel about prime rib?"

"Sounds good to me." Now I was reading double meanings into everything she said. *Stop. Just enjoy the date, or the dinner, or whatever this is.* It had been four years since Raquel died, and I'd been on only a few dates. This was starting to feel like one. "Where are we headed?"

"The Sunset Restaurant at the Cher-Ae Heights Casino. Have you been there?"

"Good choice."

The restaurant had high ceilings and a 180-degree view of the ocean. The timing was perfect—planned?—because the sun was setting. The tall pines in the foreground and Trinidad Harbor to the north had diners taking out their cell phones and grabbing postcard-like photos.

One diner made sure that Finn was in the shot. I didn't blame him. She wore an evening gown that pushed the limits of being overdressed. Of course, the bar for overdressed was pretty low in Humboldt. The dress was off the shoulder and black. The fabric was stretchy and emphasized her timeless hourglass figure.

We both ordered the prime rib special, and she let me choose the wine. If she remembered my problem with debilitating hangovers, she didn't show it. The food was excellent and got better as we burned our way through the wine. We didn't touch on the case, even though we could almost see Tepona Point from our window table.

During dessert, she squinted at me. "What's so funny?"

"Funny?"

"You smiled at something."

"Oh, nothing."

"Bunk. Spill it."

"You're not going to like it."

"Try me."

"When you talk—" I started laughing "—when you speak, the tip of your nose wiggles."

"It does not, and I don't want to talk about it." She laughed along.

We lingered, sometimes sitting in a companionable silence. I'd had most of the wine since she was driving. We watched the glow disappear from the sky, and she convinced me to try some pink frou-frou drink that included whipped cream, a pineapple section, and the obligatory umbrella. I couldn't taste the alcohol. I have no memory of what it was called.

We left the restaurant. She piled her feminine wiles on top of her persuasive skills—she was an attorney after all—and convinced me to go in and see her interesting home.

"Just a quick look, and then I've got to get home." The words felt funny in my mouth.

Her home was indeed interesting. She lived in an A-frame cabin squeezed among giant redwood trees. Her slinky black dress didn't match the rustic setting, and she must have agreed because she went in back and changed, asking me to add some more wood to the woodstove.

When I turned, I found her sitting on the plush couch holding two drinks. She'd slipped into something more comfortable but no less slinky. The soft leggings seemed painted on, and her top would have her gotten her thrown out of any courtroom in the world.

"Uh, no, Sibyl, I've had enough to drink already."

"There's very little alcohol in this. I don't think you'll even taste it. It's called a pearl diver. Just take a sip."

The firelight reflected off her hair, and I couldn't take my eyes off the curve at the nape of her neck. How did she do that?

One sip turned into another. Then one tiny kiss turned into another.

Chapter Eighteen

I WOKE NAKED IN Finn's bed, all the covers on the floor. "Finn? *Gah!*" Even the whisper of her name set off a scream of pain from my hair to my fingertips. I lay there paralyzed, trying to reconstruct the previous evening. *I got nothing.*

Wait a second. The sun was shining through the redwoods. *What time is it?* She didn't have a clock radio by the bed. I had to get up no matter how much it hurt. I got myself to a sitting position on the side of the bed and waited for the wave of agony to recede a bit.

I pressed my palms against my ears. "Finn—*Gah!*"

Where were my clothes? Not in the bedroom. I stood and had a thought. I picked up the glass from my side of the bed then reached over and took hers. I sniffed each. *Goddamn it!* Mine smelled of alcohol; hers did not. And had Finn stolen my clothes, making me a prisoner?

I stumbled down the steep stairs from the loft. I was sure I'd seen a wall clock down there, now there was nothing but a light space on the wall. There. My pants. I picked them up. *Phew.* My phone was in the back pocket. Apparently, Finn hadn't crossed the line into theft.

Aargh! 8:30. I had to be in court in thirty minutes. I had no cell phone coverage. I couldn't find a landline phone—*hidden?*

A flood of helplessness washed over me. Instant depression. I'd been a fool. *Stop! You know your perception of the world is skewed when you're depressed. Alcohol makes it worse.*

I can do this. I slapped my face then gathered my clothes, finding everything but my underwear and one sock. I put on a pair of Finn's socks instead and went commando. I would have to go straight to court. I combed my hair, but what could I do about my whiskers? They made me look like a homeless wino. I rummaged through her bathroom drawers and found a cordless Lady Remington. I stuffed it in my pocket and ran out the door. On the street I got my bearings. I was in the hills of Arcata.

I went to a neighbor's house and offered a hundred dollars for a ride into Redwood Point. He slammed the door. I didn't blame him. Probably went to his phone to call the police.

I started jogging down the hill and spun around when I heard a car coming. I waved my hands over my head, and the driver stopped and opened the passenger window. *What to say?*

"I've been drugged and kidnapped, and I need to get to the police station in Redwood Point." The police station was in the same building as the courthouse.

The man, heavyset with a white beard, thought for a moment, then said, "Ah, what the hell. Get in."

"Thank you."

I opened the door and he swept soda cans, bug spray, and rolled-up newspapers from the passenger seat. I sat down, and we were off.

"What really happened?" He fanned his hand in front of his face. "If you was drugged, it was with booze."

I gave him the full story—the true story—while using Finn's shaver on my beard.

"She the redhead? Lives in the A-frame?"

"Yeah."

"Wow. She can kidnap me anytime. There are some breath mints around here somewhere. And some deodorant. Help yourself."

It took a while, but I found the mints and a half-used stick of deodorant. Almost blind with the pain of my hangover, I put five mints in my mouth and slathered on the Old Spice deodorant. As soon as we had coverage, I checked the phone messages, all variants of *Where the hell are you?* I replied to Jen: *Ten minutes!*

"Hey, I recognize you now. You're that lawyer on TV. That murder trial. Your tie's crooked, by the way."

He dropped me at the courthouse. I gave him my thanks and a twenty for the toiletries and fashion advice. 9:05.

I ran up the stairs and collected myself in front of the doors to Courtroom 4. My pain level hadn't dropped below eleven. It made it hard to think. The drugged-and-kidnapped excuse wasn't going to fly with Stormy Stevens. My top goal was to not throw up.

I took one final breath and pushed in. Jen had her eyes on the doors, and her relief was palpable. The judge's bench was empty. What had happened?

I shuffled up the aisle. I leaned over Finn, almost puking on her. "You're going to jail for this."

She looked straight ahead.

I sat down between Jen and Carly. Rubbing my head with both hands, I took shallow breaths. *Don't vomit.* "Where's the judge?"

Jen spoke, making sure that Carly could see her lips. "She had some emergency. She'll be here soon. You lucked out. What happened?"

I leaned back so Carly could see my lips. "It's all Finn's doing. I'll tell you later. Is there something here I could throw up in?"

"Seriously?"

"Yes."

"I'll get something. You can start without me." Jen hurried down the aisle and out of the courtroom.

Carly was writing furiously. She was leaning down with her hand over her face. *F: no they'll ? through it. C: I don't care. Without ? ? bitch will walk. F: It's all your ? I want no part ? ?. I'll ? I knew nothing. C: Fine. You don't know a thing. This ? work.*

I followed her gaze, and I figured it out. Carly was speech-reading Finn and Crawford. I nodded.

I looked at the words and filled in the blanks: *They'll see through it. Without this we're sunk. I'll say I knew nothing.*

Jen returned with a plastic bag and some candies. "This is ginger candy. Suck on it."

"Do I smell like alcohol?"

She waggled her hand. "A little."

"All rise."

After the preliminaries, Finn stood and went to the lectern looking fresh and rested. Not a hair was out of place. I recalled that at the restaurant she had taken that frou-frou drink with her to the ladies room. It had puzzled me at the time, but she must have poured it down the sink.

She announced, "The People call Ms. Wendy Heron."

Jen and I looked over the witness list. Yes, she was there, highlighted as someone Louella was investigating.

Ms. Heron was brought into the courtroom through a side door. She wore prison clothing, orange top and pants with an elastic waistband.

Carly stiffened.

Oh crap! I wrote, *Cellmate?* on my pad, and Carly nodded. At that point, the conversation between Finn and Crawford made sense.

Finn led the woman, Ms. Heron, through the standard introductory questions, then asked, "Can you tell the court what Ms. Romero signed to you?"

Heron spoke clearly, but with what I call a deaf accent. Some people might mistake it for a speech impediment. For example, the word "first" might sound like "firsht." It was monotonic and throaty, the results of not being able to hear her own voice when she was young. The external components of her cochlear implant made a little bulge in her hair behind her left ear.

"Carly was crying, and she said that she felt awful bad because she'd pushed her husband off a cliff, and he was dead."

By the time she'd finished her sentence, Carly had written *NO* on my pad.

I stood and, against my better judgment, shouted, "Your Honor, they can't be serious." My skull exploded with pain and my stomach convulsed. I pushed my fingers against my mouth. I looked over to Finn. *If she's embarrassed, she's hiding it well.* Before last night, I'd never have believed that she could stoop to this level.

Storm clouds dropped over Judge Stevens's face, and she slammed her gavel down. "Mr. Goodlove, you will *not* raise your voice in my courtroom. I'll see counsel in my chambers."

It took a few minutes for Judge Stevens to hobble back to her chambers. Finn, Jen, and I sat in the judge's worn visitor chairs.

"Mr. Goodlove?"

"Your Honor, this stinks of the worst kind of fraud. It's the oldest trick in the book. No doubt it will turn out that Ms. Heron, wherever she came from, has some sentence pending that will be significantly reduced because of her testimony. Even if my client had anything to do with this event—we can barely call it a crime at this point—she'd never have said anything like that to a stranger. I told her not to speak to anyone, and she has told me that she said no such thing."

"Ms. Finn?"

She took a breath. "I'll look into it. Detective Crawford just filled me in last night."

"Yet she was on your witness list weeks ago."

Not having a gavel, the judge slapped her hand on her desk. "You will not address opposing counsel, Mr. Goodlove. You talk with me."

"I'm sorry, Your Honor. This thing makes me so angry." I was itching to show her the transcript of Finn's conversation with Crawford that Carly had overheard. But that would be the end of our ability to eavesdrop on them. Also, I became distracted because I'd just figured out how I could get access to Louella's report.

"All right. I agree this does not pass the smell test. But if you had Ms. Heron on your witness list, why were you unprepared for her testimony?"

"My investigator got very sick and was unable to get her report to me." I worried that revealing that someone had tried to kill Louella would result in a mistrial. With access to her report, combined with the theory that was growing in my mind, I felt we had a chance to win this thing. "Your Honor, may I ask for a recess for several days?"

"We have already had too many delays in this trial. Ms. Finn?"

"Your Honor, he had this witness on his list." Finn put bored annoyance into the tone of her voice. "He's had adequate time to figure out how to spin what his client said to her."

I said, "Your Honor—"

Stevens held her hand up, doing her traffic cop impersonation again. "We will stand in recess until tomorrow at nine. Will that give you adequate time to prepare, Mr. Goodlove?"

Maybe. "Yes, Your Honor. Thank you."

The judge pointed to Finn. "If I find you've engaged in any shenanigans or that Detective Crawford has, with your blessings, your career as a prosecutor will be finished. Finished! Do you understand?"

"Yes, Your Honor."

"Is there anything you wish to say now?"

"No, ma'am."

An hour later, Jen and I parked in front of Louella's house. I'd put on a fresh set of clothes then brushed my teeth and shaved. I didn't feel like a new man. I felt like an old one with irritable bowel syndrome, but I looked respectable.

"I still don't see how you're going to get the report, boss. I knew—know—Louella, and I can assure you that she encrypted her laptop."

"You'll get a kick out of this." I looked around. No one was watching us.

The screaming green sticker on the door read, "THESE PREMISES HAVE BEEN SEALED BY THE REDWOOD POINT POLICE DEPARTMENT PURSUANT TO SECTION 435, ADMINISTRATIVE CODE. ALL PERSONS ARE FORBIDDEN TO ENTER UNLESS AUTHORIZED BY THE POLICE DEPARTMENT."

I unlocked the door with the key Louella had given me years ago, then I led Jen up to Louella's office.

I shot my cuffs like a magician. "Watch this." Around the back of her antique desk, I pushed and prodded.

"What the hell are you doing? Looking for a secret—oh!"

I'd found the unlocking trick, and a hidden door flipped down. *Please be in there.* I reached in and pulled out Louella's laptop and unplugged it. She'd shown me the compartment once—it had a power cord inside.

"Ta-da." I put the computer on the desk and opened it up. In the center of the display sat a text entry box with "Enter Password" above it.

"Right," Jen said. "I don't want to say, 'I told you so,' but ..."

I closed the secret compartment and winked at her. The act of closing one eye sent a spasm of pain through my head. "Now we go to the hospital."

"Is Louella conscious?"

Louella had been moved to a semiprivate room, shared with another comatose patient. I was still on her visitor list, and the guard didn't object when I took Jen in to see her. I didn't know of any regulations about bringing electronics into the room, but just in case, I'd hidden her laptop under my jacket. After talking to Louella for bit, I pulled out the laptop, opened it up, and put Louella's index finger on the fingerprint reader.

Jen smiled. "Of course. Why didn't I think of that?"

Nothing happened. She knew that police could force you to provide your fingerprint to unlock a laptop, but they couldn't force you to give them the password. *Damn!*

"Try a different finger."

"No, everyone uses their index finger."

Apparently not. When I put Louella's middle finger on the reader, the screen changed. We were in. Maybe she liked to give her computer the finger.

"Let's go," I said.

"Hold on." Jen took the laptop and had it learn our fingerprints. Smart.

I gave her a kiss on the cheek and did the same to Louella. "Hang in there, my good friend. I love you, Louella."

Back at the office, I copied the report to our laptops, and Jen and I pored over it. It was even more than we could have hoped for.

Chapter Nineteen

SOMETHING WOKE ME UP in the middle of the night. I looked at the clock radio. 3:14 a.m.

A crash from downstairs hit me like a slap in the face. I came fully awake. *Whoever tried to kill Louella was coming after me.* Did they know I'd gotten her final report? Impossible, only Jen and I knew that.

I didn't have a gun. All I had was a Maglite flashlight. The big black type that cops use. With four D cell batteries, the thing was heavy enough to kill someone. I stepped from the bed, clearing my Eustachian tubes so I could hear more clearly. Mercifully, my hangover had finally dissipated.

I tiptoed to the wall and pulled the flashlight from its holder. The phrase, *He brought a flashlight to a gunfight* ran through my head. Maybe that would go on my tombstone. I started toward my bedroom door, when it swung open, and the ceiling light came on.

"Dad! Dad, listen. You're gonna love this. You'll never guess what I found in Dundon's house."

"Toby?"

"You're not listening, Dad."

"Why aren't you in the hospital? What happened?"

He was talking a mile a minute. "Oh they have lousy security there and it was easy for me to break out and I just waited until someone went out the double doors at the end of the ward and then I caught the door before it closed all the way but that's not important now this is."

Toby still wore the psych ward hospital scrubs. *How did he get here?*

"Hey, buddy. Sit down on the bed and take a deep breath. Slow down."

He took a breath, but it probably broke the speed record for deep breaths. In, out, talk. "I thought back to how Bridget was having an affair with Uncle Angelo, so I broke into her house—"

"You *what?*"

"I broke into her house and looked around. I went into a back room, and you know what I found? I found this big kinda dummy thing, like a man, only it was made of like branches and rocks held together with twine or something. It was heavy. Isn't that weird? Do you think that has anything to do with Uncle Angelo's death? Because I think it has to."

With what I knew from Louella's report, it wasn't actually that weird. Well, it was weird, but I understood what was going on.

"Buddy, you shouldn't have done that, but it was helpful. Can you do something for me? Will you let me take you back to the hospital?"

I got him readmitted. No one had even realized he was gone. I didn't get back to sleep until six.

* * *

The audience had doubled since news of the jailhouse snitch broke. Fine with me.

At the start of my cross, I asked, "Ms. Heron, do you collect Get out of Jail Free cards?"

Finn stood, about to object, then sat.

"I don't understand." With Heron's deaf dialect, "*understand*" sounded like "*undershtand.*"

"Well, it seems that you've gotten out of jail a number of times in exchange for your testimony."

"Objection. Mr. Goodlove isn't testifying here."

"Sustained."

"Do you remember being in jail in Las Vegas ten months ago?"

"Not really."

"You don't remember being incarcerated for passing bad checks?"

"Oh, yeah, I remember. But they let me out."

"Ah, good. And why did they dismiss the charges and let you go?"

"'Cause I didn't do it. Duh."

Finn popped up. "Objection. This line of questioning is clearly beyond the scope of direct."

Nice try. "Your Honor, this is related to—"

She held up her hand toward me. "Overruled."

"Ms. Heron, do you remember that before you were released, you testified against your cellmate?"

"I might have."

I introduced a trial transcript into evidence and asked her to read the highlighted line out loud.

"Uh … 'Mary said she poisoned her boyfriend because he was cheating on her and the motherfucker deserved to die, but she had only meant for him to get real sick.'"

According to a report by the Center on Wrongful Convictions at Northwestern University, jailhouse-snitch testimony is the leading cause of wrongful convictions in murder cases.

"Had you met with the prosecutor before being put in the cell with that woman—Mary?"

"I may have."

"Please answer yes or no."

"Yes, I think so."

"And did he suggest to you that your charges would be dismissed if she said anything incriminating and you testified about it?"

"It's how the system works, right? I made a deal, right?"

"Did he tell you what Mary was accused of and what kind of testimony might get your charges dismissed?"

She shrugged. "Yeah, something like that."

I introduced the court record showing that Heron's cellmate was exonerated, that she had been proven innocent of the charge of manslaughter. I also led Ms. Heron through another instance in which her testimony was used in court and later found to be false. I had planned to spend more time on the fact that she'd obviously been transferred to our jail because they needed someone who understood ASL and that Crawford had coached her on exactly what he wanted her to say. But I saw it in the jurors' faces: They got it. And they were getting bored. Can't have *that*.

I wrapped things up, confident that Crawford's jailhouse snitch had been convincingly discredited. The defense table was a happier place than the prosecution table.

The prosecution rested. I made a motion to have the charges dismissed, but it was denied. Apparently, Judge Stevens was unwilling to ignore the eyewitness testimony.

Over the weekend, Finn offered a plea to manslaughter, with a recommended sentence of eight years. We turned it down. Tax day, April 15, was our day to present our case. Finally. We began by attacking the reliability of the eyewitness, Ms. Yvette Dowzer.

Our expert witness, a Dr. Hiram Bosch, had PhDs in psychology and criminology and taught at USC. He didn't come cheap, but he was well respected, and, most importantly, came off well on the stand. Jen handled the direct examination.

After running him through his impressive qualifications, she asked. "Dr. Bosch, what does science tell us about the reliability of eyewitnesses?"

He adjusted the microphone. "In general, it's very poor. Many people have been convicted based on eyewitness testimony that has turned out to be mistaken."

"Isn't that surprising?"

"Not at all. The human brain isn't like a video recorder. It's not like cueing up an old video and reviewing it. Instead, our visual memories are reconstructed. My colleague, Dr. Elizabeth F. Loftus, likens it to putting puzzle pieces together. All too often, the pieces are put together in the wrong way, or they've been overwritten with some different pieces, so to speak."

Jen put a confused look on her face. She had some good acting skills. "But surely, doctor, if the witness is certain about the identity of the person she saw, that's much more reliable."

"Sadly, no. Many studies have shown that witnesses who are highly confident are no more reliable than those who are uncertain of their identification."

"Why is that sad?"

"Because jurors give more weight to witnesses who are sure of what they saw."

I glanced back at Ms. Dowzer, the eyewitness. She seemed fascinated.

Jen did a great job. She hit all the important points yet didn't bore the jurors. I wanted to give her a kiss when she came back to the defense table.

The judge said, "Ms. Finn?"

Finn stood. *Why is she so confident?*

"Dr. Bosch, have you read the testimony of Ms. Dowzer in this case?"

"I have."

"I've learned—and I hope you'll correct me if I'm wrong—that eyewitnesses are less reliable if they are under stress at the time of the event."

"Yes, that's true."

"Did you get the impression that Ms. Dowzer was under a lot of stress when she identified the defendant?"

"No."

"She was going for a walk when this happened. Do you think she was under any stress at all?"

"Probably not."

"Isn't it true that she was probably as unstressed as anyone could be?"

"Possibly. I have no way of knowing what she was thinking about at the time."

"That's fair. Do you think she was under stress when Detective Crawford asked her to identify the defendant from photographs?"

"I can't say for sure."

"I've read that the presence of weapons is distracting and stressful and decreases the reliability of witnesses. Is that right?"

"Very true."

"Was there a weapon involved when Ms. Dowzer saw the defendant?"

"There was not."

"Is it true that a disparity in race between the witness and the person he or she identifies decreases witness reliability?"

"Yes."

"But in this case the witness and the person she saw were both Caucasian," Finn said.

"Probably."

"Probably?"

"Well, from the testimony, the witness only saw the person's face for a brief instant, and it was obscured by the hood of a sweatshirt. She could very well be mistaken about the race. Brevity of observation correlates inversely with reliability."

Score a point for our side if the jurors understood.

Obviously, Finn didn't want to end on a down note. "But it's your testimony that the reliability didn't suffer because of stress, the presence of a weapon, or—"

Jen stood. "Objection. Asked and answered."

"Sustained."

"No further questions," Finn said.

"Redirect, Ms. Shek?"

I whispered in Jen's ear and she nodded.

She stood up. "Dr. Bosch, I heard you say that brevity of observation correlates inversely with reliability." She smiled. "I'm having trouble wrapping my head around that. What the heck does it mean?"

"Yes, sorry. It means that the shorter the time during which the witness sees the subject, the less reliable the identification."

"Ah, I see. That means that in this case when Ms. Dowzer said, and I quote, 'Well, I do admit that I only got a very quick look at her face. Just a flash, you know,' it means that because her observation was very brief, it's not reliable."

I grimaced a bit.

"Well, not exactly. I'd say that because it was very brief, it is *less* reliable."

"No more questions."

Jen whispered, "Sorry about that, chief" when she sat.

"No big deal. Nice job."

My turn. I confirmed that the crabber was not in the room. I'd given instructions that he be excluded from the courtroom until I brought him in to testify, but I wanted to make sure. Then I called the head of the local Coast Guard station and ran him through his qualifications with regard to ocean currents.

I put a nautical chart on an easel. I like to get witnesses away from the stand. It lets them better relate to the jurors. I got permission to approach him and handed him a pointer. "Can you tell us about the prevailing currents in our area?"

He illustrated the currents with his pointer. He went into a little too much detail, and the jurors were barely hanging on. I stopped him.

"I'm confused, sir. You've shown that the currents are moving north from Tepona Point, and yet Mr. Rozetti discovered the body to the south, straight out from the Redwood Point jetty. Maybe the currents were different that day in December?"

He laughed. "No, they couldn't have been that different. The ocean doesn't work that way. Besides, we have buoy data that shows that the body would have drifted north."

"Now I'm really confused. If the body would have drifted north, how could it have been discovered to the south?"

Finn jumped to her feet. "Objection as to relevance. We know the body was found where it was found. Who cares where it was found? Mr. Goodlove is just blowing smoke."

"Mr. Goodlove, care to enlighten us?" Stevens seemed a little more lively than usual.

"Your Honor, the relevance will become clear soon."

"How soon?"

"After a few more witnesses."

"Okay, I'll allow it."

I repeated the question. "If the body would have drifted north, how could it have been discovered south?"

"It couldn't."

"Excuse me?" *Am I laying it on too thick?*

"There is simply no way that the body could have drifted south like that."

"What if someone had picked it up and taken it south?" Now I *was* blowing smoke. I didn't want Finn to know where I was going.

"That's the only way it could have gotten to where that crabber reported seeing it."

"Maybe the crabber wasn't where he thought he was."

The Coast Guard officer laughed. "He'd have to have been thirty or forty miles north of where he thought he was. If his boat could travel at six knots, that would have been five or more hours of motoring. In each direction. He would have remembered. No way."

"No further questions."

Finn didn't cross-examine.

We next called an expert on how bodies float. He splashed more cold water, so to speak, on the testimony of the crabber. Jen went through it quickly but caught the high points. It was unlikely that the body had been floating faceup as Rozetti described. To have the body flip over and sink immediately was also unlikely.

"So to sum up," she said, "you find the testimony of the crabber, Mr. Rozetti, to be suspect?"

"In the extreme. Dead bodies, and I've dealt with a lot, just don't act that way."

"Thank you."

I'd selfishly saved the next witness for myself, a Dr. Bloome, whom we'd flown out from Illinois. He was an expert on DNA and tissue evidence in general.

Finn stipulated to his expertise, and I got to the meat of the matter, almost rubbing my hands in anticipation. "Dr. Bloome, did you get a chance to analyze the material the RPPD supplied you?"

"I did."

"It was evidence taken from the crabber's boat hook, is that correct?"

"It is."

"And did your analysis show that the DNA on that boat hook belonged to Mr. Angelo Romero?"

"It did, to an astronomically high probability."

"Unless Mr. Romero had a twin brother."

"True. Did he?"

I laughed. "Not that we know of. Now, was the sample they sent you consistent with Mr. Romero having been floating in salt water for four days?"

"Well, that might be misleading."

I had been pacing back and forth a little to the amount allowed in the well, and at that point I froze. "Wait. What? Misleading? I don't understand."

"It's true that the sample had been in salt water. But it had not been in the Pacific Ocean."

"I don't get it." I turned slightly, so the jurors would see my Oscar-worthy performance, and frowned. "Was it in the Atlantic or something? The Indian Ocean?"

He laughed. "No, it wasn't in the ocean at all. My analysis suggested that the tissue sat in a bucket of seawater taken from the harbor, perhaps, that had been sitting at a temperature higher than that of the ocean."

Adding my puzzled look to the bewildered murmuring of the courtroom, I said, "What? How could you possibly know that?"

He launched into a technical and jargon-filled explanation touching on salinity, water temperature, microbes, and so on. The jurors were curious about the plot twist in this murder mystery, but when some eyes started to glaze over, I got him to finish up.

Finn had no questions. Hopefully, she thought I was just throwing out some red herrings.

Chapter Twenty

AFTER THE LUNCH BREAK, I stood. "The defense calls Mr. Guyapi Yazzi."

Mr. Yazzi had the unmistakable look of a Native American. His black hair was parted in the middle and streamed back over his ears to a ponytail that extended down to his shoulder blades. He had dark eyes, high cheekbones, and turquoise earrings.

After he was sworn in, and before I could ask my first question, he spoke a few words in what was apparently Havasupai. After confounding the court reporter for a while, he said, "This is a traditional greeting of my people, which I am bound to give, albeit a short version."

"Thank you, Mr. Yazzi, I enjoyed that." I was sincere. It was interesting to hear a language that sounded like no other. "Could you tell us your occupation?"

"I run a tour company and school in Havasu Canyon, which includes the reservation of my people." He had a deep voice and spoke English perfectly.

"Can you tell us what you teach at this school?" *Here it comes.*

"Cliff diving."

A few murmurs sounded in the courtroom.

"That's fascinating. Can you tell me more?"

"We have some wonderful cliffs and waterfalls in my homeland. People come from around the world to learn how to jump off them and into the river safely."

"On November eleventh of last year, did a Mr. Angelo Romero come to your school?"

"He did."

"Did you teach him how to jump off a cliff?"

"I did," Yazzi said. "He was good. But he was better after my lessons."

"I see. Did you get the impression he'd done it before?"

"Yes, a little. He said he'd been to South Point on Hawaii. That's where he started learning."

"Did he want to learn fancy maneuvers? Like flips and such?"

"No, not at all. I told him he was a natural and he could be good at it, but he just wanted to be able to jump without hurting himself. It can be dangerous if you don't have a good instructor. It's a wonderful sport. I recommend it to everyone. Anyway, Angelo did it over and over, from different heights."

"Anything else?" I'd told Mr. Yazzi the general points I wanted to cover, but we hadn't done practice sessions. I wanted him to sound natural, which he did.

"He said he was going to go to La Quebrada in Mexico. That's another good cliff diving destination. They have a school there. I've been there."

"But if Mr. Romero was so good, why did he want to go to yet another school?"

"He said he needed to learn how to judge waves. There are no waves in Havasu. At the ocean, you have to jump at just the right time. If you land between the peaks of the waves, you can hit the bottom and die. That's another reason you need instruction."

Finn had no questions.

"The defense calls Mr. Wenzel Rozetti back to the stand."

The roly-poly crabber looked even more nervous than he had before. *Now I know why.*

"Mr. Rozetti, you testified that you saw the body in the ocean straight out from the jetty. It was floating faceup, but when you tried to get it to the boat using the boat hook, it flipped over. You saw the tattoo on the back of Mr. Romero's neck. You tried to get the body to the boat, but it sank. Is that about right?"

"Yeah, that's just right." His body relaxed, like, *I see, they just want to confirm what I said.* He hadn't heard any of the testimony since his.

"Why did you use the boat hook?"

He looked at me as if I'd asked why the ocean was wet. "What do you mean? To get the body, of course."

"Why not use your hands?"

"Oh, I see what you mean. No, the body was too far away."

"You couldn't have just brought the boat right up next to the body and grabbed it, tried to bring it into the boat, or tied it up?"

Finn stood. "Objection. Relevance. Where is this going? What does it matter exactly how it happened? We know the boat hook came in contact with the body."

I looked at her. *She must have caught on.*

I turned back to the judge. "Your Honor, the relevance will become apparent very soon."

Stevens pulled on her ear. "I'm going to allow it, but let's keep things moving, counselor. You may answer the question, Mr. Rozetti."

I led him through questions that made it clear the boat hook wasn't really needed.

Changing the subject, I asked, "You've said that you didn't know Mr. Romero, is that right?"

"Yes."

I shrugged and lifted my hands. "Never saw him before?"

"Maybe I've seen him. It's a small town."

"Yes, it is," I said. "You didn't work with him?"

"No. I'd have—no, I didn't."

"Have you heard of a company called DialUSA?"

The blood drained from his face. "Yes."

"I'm sorry, I couldn't hear you."

"Yes. Yes, I have."

"And did you work for them, off and on?"

He swallowed. "Yeah."

"Was this an off-the-books job?"

"No."

"Did you report these earnings on your tax returns?"

Finn stood. "Objection. Mr. Rozetti is not on trial here."

"Overruled."

"Some of them."

"Is it true that there are some bad dudes involved with that company? That they do illegal things?"

He shook his head. "I don't know anything about that."

"And yet they must have told you they weren't reporting your earnings to the IRS. Wouldn't that make them criminals?"

"Maybe."

"Mr. Rozetti, is it true that just a few days before you reported seeing Mr. Romero's body, you purchased a very expensive flat-screen TV?"

"Absolutely. Sure."

"Did you ever see Mr. Romero working at DialUSA?"

"Ah, yeah." He actually snapped his fingers. "That's where I'd seen him, yeah."

"Mr. Rozetti, had Angelo done anything to anger the bad dudes at DialUSA? The ones from out of state?"

"I don't know. How should I know that?"

I would like to have said, "*Let the court record show that Mr. Rozetti has started sweating profusely.*" I looked at the jurors. *Are they noticing?*

"Mr. Rozetti, did Angelo pay you to make it seem that he'd died by falling into the ocean so he could disappear and the bad guys would think he was dead?"

"What? No! Of course not."

"Remembering that you are under oath, did Angelo cut himself, or otherwise get some of his tissue on your boat hook, then tell you to put it in a bucket of seawater, and take it out on your boat so you could come in and give it to police to test?"

"No."

"Louder, please."

"No!"

"Did he give you a good look at his new tattoo so that you could describe it to the police as part of this whole cock-and-bull story about seeing his body out in the ocean?"

"No."

The airhorn they found at Tepona Point!

"Isn't it true that Angelo Romero is alive and well? He told you that he was going to blow an airhorn so that the surfers would look up, and then he'd jump from the cliff and make it look like he fell. He was going to time his jump with the waves so that he would survive, then he would swim in and run away. Everyone would assume he was dead, and they'd be sure of it once the DNA from your boat hook was a match. Isn't that so?"

Even the slowpokes in the courtroom got the idea at that point. I loved the murmuring.

"No. That's crazy talk. I saw his body in the ocean just like I said."

A Perry Mason moment was too much to hope for. That is, to have a witness jump up and say, "*Yes! I admit it. It's all true!*" Those don't happen in real life.

Before I got a chance to say that I was done with the witness, a bailiff banged in through the doors, rushed up the aisle, went to the bench, and handed Judge Stevens a folded note. Her eyebrows flew into the stratosphere.

"I'd like to see counsel in my chambers, right now."

As soon as we were seated, Finn started in. "Your Honor, this whole ridiculous fantasy—"

The judge gave her the traffic cop treatment. I didn't even want to look at Finn.

Stevens took a breath. "Mr. Angelo Romero's body has turned up."

I was speechless.

"Apparently it washed up on a remote beach south of Crescent City, in a protected cave. Some hikers found it. The medical examiner up there just completed a quick DNA test and confirmed it was Mr. Romero. We're keeping this under wraps until an examination is performed, but it's likely him."

Crescent City was to the north, confirming the Coast Guard officer's assessment of the currents.

"I hate to do this," the judge said, "but I'm going to declare a mistrial."

"No!"

She frowned. "But, Mr. Goodlove, you said, not ten minutes ago, that Mr. Romero was alive and well."

"True. I was clearly wrong. But my theory, which I have a lot of confidence in, can't be rejected because of this. He planned to be alive and well, but his plans went awry. I think I can explain why that happened. We do not want to go through this again. The state doesn't want to pay for yet another trial."

"Ms. Finn?"

"May I confer with Mr. Goodlove?"

"You may not."

I suspected Finn wanted a deal. A quid pro quo: She wouldn't oppose a mistrial, and I wouldn't bring up her misconduct. That would have been a tough decision for me. I was glad I didn't have to make it.

"Ms. Finn, will you be cross-examining Mr. Rozetti?"

"No," Finn said.

"How many more witnesses will you need, Mr. Goodlove?"

"One, only. We can finish today, with closing arguments tomorrow."

The judge sighed. "Okay. Let's git 'er done."

Apparently Judge Stevens was a fan of Larry the Cable Guy.

Before stepping to the lectern, I looked over the spectators. *Nicole!* My daughter must have taken time off from law school to come watch her dad. I smiled at her and winked.

At the lectern, I said, "The defense calls Ms. Bridget Dundon to the stand."

I'd excluded Bridget from the courtroom for everything that followed her testimony; I'd had a feeling she was involved. I'd also sat Carly down and told her it was Bridget who'd had the long-term affair with her husband. She'd freaked but not quite as badly as I'd expected. She gave me her word that she'd keep herself under control, but she tensed significantly when her disloyal friend walked up to the witness stand.

I didn't waste any time. I signed my questions to her, and the ASL translator converted them into English for the rest of the people in the courtroom. "Ms. Dundon, were you having an affair with the deceased, Mr. Angelo Romero?" Did she know that Angelo was, in the words of the Munchkin coroner, most sincerely dead?

"No … yes." She made the "sorry" sign again, but Carly kept her eyes on her hands in front of her.

Time for the shotgun blast between the eyes. "Were you part of Angelo's scheme to fake his own death?"

Bang! Her head jerked back. She'd turned white as a Beluga whale. "No! What? I don't know what you're talking about," she signed.

"The bad guys were after him. He thought they had a contract out," I said. "You two schemed to fake his death then run off and live together. Take on new identities. Did you suggest that he throw a dummy off the cliff, but he said he could jump without killing himself?"

Jen and Carly looked at me like, *Where is this coming from?* But Bridget's expression said to me, and perhaps to the jury, *How did he know that?*

She tried to disguise her shock as confusion. "I don't know what you're talking about."

I asked a question to which I didn't know the answer. It was safe, though. I couldn't think of an answer that would hurt us. "Were you there with Angelo when he jumped off the cliff?"

Before she answered, a shriek came from the spectator seats. I spun around.

Ms. Dowzer stood and pointed at Bridget. "She's the one I saw. It was *her!*"

I looked at Bridget then at my sister. *Of course.* I hadn't noticed it because I'd grown up with Carly, but to a stranger, the two women looked remarkably similar. And they both had Bizet hoodies.

Why hadn't I figured that out? I'd had all the pieces. When the anonymous woman told Carly about the affair, she'd written, *I thought it was you, but when I got closer, I saw it was someone else.* When telling me of the affair, Toby had said, "I always thought men had affairs with women who are really different from their wives. I guess that's not always true."

Pandemonium. Stevens rapped her gavel multiple times. I was hoping she'd say, "Order! Order in the court!" because I'd never heard that in real life, only in movies, but that didn't happen.

Then I got the hunch that put all the puzzle pieces together. Angelo's body tumbled through the air, as the surfer had testified, but he hadn't learned how to do flips. And there had been a delay between the sound of the airhorn and Angelo's fall. *Should I go for it?*

"Ms. Dundon," I said, "Angelo's body has been found. Not just some fake DNA evidence that you and he cooked up. Your boyfriend is dead. Isn't it true that you were with Angelo when he was ready to jump off Tepona Point? He blew the airhorn then hesitated. You thought he was chickening out, so you helped him."

"Objection! Leading."

"Sustained."

I kept going. "You pushed him. But he wasn't chickening out. He was waiting for a big wave, for just the right time to jump. But you pushed him, so he fell at the wrong time, in between wave peaks. He was killed when he slammed into the rocks. Isn't that what happened?"

She buried her head in the hands. Her crying sounded subtly different from a hearing person's sobs.

Then it happened: Bridget nodded.

Judge Stevens said, "Let the record show that the witness nodded. Ms. Dundon, can you please answer with a yes or no?"

But of course Bridget couldn't hear what the judge was asking her to do.

I guess Perry Mason moments do sometimes happen in real life.

Chapter Twenty-One

JUDGE STEVENS HAD HEARD enough. She dismissed the charges and cracked her gavel. With that sound, Carly's nightmare was over.

We celebrated in the office with pizza and champagne, rehashing the whole trial.

"What the hell was all that about a dummy?" Carly asked.

"Dummy?" I frowned but couldn't keep the smile off my face.

"C'mon, boss, spill it," Jen said.

"I had some information from a secret source that there was a dummy in Dundon's house."

"Louella didn't break in, did she?"

"No. The dummy was made with sticks and rocks tied together with fishing nets. Throw it off the cliff, and from a distance, say three hundred meters, it would look like a person falling. A regular mannequin wouldn't work. It might wash up on the shore, and the jig would be up. But this dummy would sink and break up in the surf."

Jen looked up at the ceiling. "But one of them decided there was a better way."

Carly signed, "That would be Angelo."

We all looked at her.

"Angelo always wanted to do things the risky way," she said. "It's why he was always involved in one barely legal scheme or another. Will Bridget go to jail?"

"She'll likely be charged with involuntary manslaughter. She didn't intend to kill him, she was probably just trying to help. Unless she was mad. Like, 'C'mon, you big pussy, just jump already.' But in any case, what she did was inherently reckless, and she would have known that. Maybe, because she's deaf, Angelo wasn't able to communicate quickly enough that he was waiting for the right moment to jump."

Nicole said, "But what they did was part of the commission of a crime."

"What crime was that?" I asked.

"It's got to be illegal to fake your own death, right?"

"Surprisingly, no. But if it turns out that Bridget stood to get some money from a life insurance policy, for example, that would be fraud."

Carly signed, "I'm going to push *her* off a fucking cliff."

I didn't think it was funny.

Louella woke from her coma a few days after the trial was over. Jen and I drove to St. Joe's to see her.

A full recovery was out of the question. Because of the delay between the heart attack and the treatment, she'd lost too much cardiac muscle. There would be some improvement, but she'd always have a weak heart. Gail said they were looking into the possibility of a heart transplant.

Irrationally, I kept wishing I had tried harder to make her quit smoking. Jen said that she'd never have listened.

At the bedside, we had to lean in close to hear her.

"Is the trial still going on?" she whispered.

I smiled. "You're supposed to say, 'Where am I?'"

She shook her head. "Already did that. What happened?"

"It's all over, thanks to you." I filled her in.

She told us about the intruders.

"The FBI is rolling up the DialUSA operation. They caught the guy that shot at you."

A nurse told us that Louella had to rest, and we said our goodbyes. Hopefully not our final goodbyes.

Up at the psych ward, I visited with Toby. He was beginning to respond to the administration of lithium, and the docs felt it was a clear sign that he had bipolar disorder. He was emotionally flat, and his hands shook, but his doctor assured me that would improve as they dialed in the correct dosage. He'd be released in a week.

Crawford lost his job but wouldn't face criminal charges for his suborning of perjury. He moved out of the area. Finn denied any knowledge of the fraud, so I set up a conference in Judge Stevens's chambers.

As soon as we sat, Finn said, "Goodlove is just out to get me, Your Honor. I don't know what kind of grudge he's got. Of *course* I didn't know anything about what that sleazeball Crawford was doing."

Stevens sighed and turned to me. "I tend to agree with you, Mr. Goodlove, but there's simply no evidence that Ms. Finn was in on it."

"May I read a transcript?"

"A transcript?"

"This is what Ms. Finn and Detective Crawford said right before they called the jailhouse snitch."

I read from the sheet in my hand:

> "Finn: No. They'll see through it.

> "Crawford: I don't care. Without Heron's testimony, the bitch will walk.

> "Finn: It's all your doing. I want no part of it. I'll say I knew nothing.

> "Crawford: Fine. You don't know a thing. This will work."

I'd had to fill in some of the words Carly had been unable to speech-read, but it was close enough. The dramatic flush of Finn's pale face, seen by the judge, was as good as a confession.

"Where did you get this?" Stevens demanded.

"My sister overheard it." I put bunny quotes around the word "overheard."

"I don't understand—ah. Lipreading."

"Exactly."

That was the last I saw of the beautiful and evil Sibyl Finn. The notes in her termination statement would follow her wherever she went. If she switched to criminal defense, the episode would help her: Crooks love a sneaky lawyer who bends the rules.

There was no point in bringing up the fact that she'd seduced me and drugged me with alcohol, taking advantage of my susceptibility to devastating hangovers. That was all on me.

At least one good thing came out of the whole episode: Carly and I were close again. We made plans to go surfing on Tuesdays and have dinner together every Sunday with Toby and, on holidays, Nicole. A real family.

I took Jen to the Sunset Restaurant, timing it perfectly with the setting of the sun. We got a pleasant surprise while waiting for our table.

"Look who's here." I gestured with my head, smiling.

In a sunken part of the dining area, a young family had just been served their main course. Their cute, pigtailed pixie of a daughter sat in a high chair, fussing about something.

"Isn't that ...? Wow, what a surprise."

I shrugged.

"Don't tell me you foresaw that?"

"If you'd seen Hortense in her dad's lap at the settlement meeting, you'd have foreseen it, too. Molly loved Horace's identical twin, so why wouldn't she fall in love with Horace?"

I decided to leave the family alone since they might have been embarrassed by the commotion their daughter was causing, but later, after Jen and I had ordered, Molly came to our table.

"No, don't get up." She squatted down next to me, her hand on my forearm. "I don't want to interrupt your dinner, but I wanted to thank you for the way you handled our dispute."

"I'm glad it turned out the way it did."

"Yes, thanks to you." She glanced over at Jen. "Horace and I are going to be married this June. We'd be honored if you and your beautiful wife would come to the wedding."

"Thank you. We'd enjoy that."

After she left, Jen laughed. "Did you forget the part that goes, 'That's not my wife, that's my law partner'?"

I put my napkin in my lap. "I figured she was already embarrassed because she was interrupting us. Why complicate things?"

Jen and I had the prime rib and lingered over a second bottle of red wine.

"Boss, I have a question about when the trial started, when you came in late."

"Okay."

"You seemed really ... I don't know, down."

"Depressed."

"Yeah. Are you doing okay?"

"No problem. I'm good."

She squinted and looked at me sideways. "C'mon, boss. Be straight with me."

I rubbed the back of my neck and watched the glow disappearing from the western horizon. "Jen, it's still a struggle, but I'm okay, really. I guess it's like being an alcoholic." I held up my wineglass. "One day at a time."

"But don't think about it too much."

"Don't what?"

Jen described Louella's philosophy of life: Don't spend too much time examining whether you're happy or not.

I chuckled. "Did she quote George Carlin? Just get up, go to work, go to bed, then do it all over again?"

"Yeah, okay, I guess she's told you that, too. But promise me you won't hide it. From me, anyway. Deal?"

"*Ach.* I don't want to do that. After a while it would be like, 'Are you okay today, boss? What about now?'"

A flash of anger crossed her face. "I would never be like that. You know me. Just promise that you won't hide it, okay?"

I said nothing.

"Do you remember one day when I came into your office and you had your forehead on your desk. You pretended that you'd dropped something."

"I didn't fool you?"

"I knew you were in trouble, but I ignored it. I told myself I was too busy, and you were my boss and you could handle it yourself. I've felt bad about that for years."

"I *did* handle it," I said.

"But I might have *done something,* and I didn't. Help me feel better by promising you'll let me know when I can help."

I nodded. "Deal."

"Good. Did you and Finn do it?"

Bang. Abrupt change of subject. I'd seen Jen do that to catch a witness off guard. "You mean—" I smiled and made the ASL sign for "sex," two peace signs—or bunny rabbits—bumping one another.

"Whatever that means," she said. "Did you two have sex or not?"

"I don't remember."

"Objection. Unresponsive."

"It wasn't unresponsive. I really don't remember. Yeah, I woke up in her bed, naked. But maybe she just took off my clothes to slow me down in the morning."

"C'mon, boss."

"No, really."

"Can't you tell, the next morning, if you've ..." She made vague gestures toward my nether regions.

I laughed. "I had other things on my mind. I was naked, looking for my clothes, and my twin sister was on trial for murder starting in half an hour. I wasn't concerned with analyzing ..." I made my own vague gestures toward my lap.

She looked out the window, apparently unsatisfied.

After a while I took her hand. "Jen, remember when you mentioned that you thought a lot of women were interested in me in ... 'that way'?"

She didn't reply.

"And I said something like, 'You too?' and you blushed?"

She was blushing again. "I don't really recall."

I stammered a bit, even though we'd been partners for years. "Jen, I've realized that I have feelings for you that I didn't, uh, realize." *Garrett Goodlove, the silver-tongued attorney.* "I'd, uh, I think I'd like to pursue that. A romantic relationship. What do you think?"

Her eyes met mine.

Aargh! I hate it when she gives me that inscrutable look.

Acknowledgments

I'm so grateful for the help I've had with this book.

Many thanks to Margaret Klaw, author of the delightful book, *Keeping It Civil: The Case of the Pre-nup and the Porsche & Other True Accounts from the Files of a Family Lawyer*, for both inspiring the donor insemination subplot and allowing me to appropriate some text from a contract described in her book. The first sentence of *Conclusive Evidence* also comes from her book. Special thanks to attorneys Candace Elliott Person and James P. Frederick for uncovering and helping me correct some legal errors.

My buddies at Early-Retirement.org helped me hash out some plot ideas. Special thanks to BestWifeEver and Robert M. Ring.

Allison Maruska, author of *The Fourth Descendant*, provided her usual insightful tips.

I had a great beta-reader crew, as usual. Thanks to my wonderful wife, Lena, who is always the first reader for my books. Thanks as well to Navtej Nandra, Steven Lord, Gail Summerville, Manie Kilian, Linda Johnson and others.

My copy editor, Julie MacKenzie from FreeRangeEditorial.com always does a consistently wonderful job. She's a pleasure to work with, and I'm getting tired of looking for new ways to praise her.

Also by Al Macy

Becoming a Great Sight-Reader—or Not! Learn from my Quest for Piano Sight-Reading Nirvana
Drive, Ride, Repeat: The Mostly True Account of a Cross-Country Car and Bicycle Adventure

Contact Us: A Jake Corby Sci-Fi Thriller
The Antiterrorist: A Jake Corby Sci-Fi Thriller
The Universe Next Door: A Jake Corby Sci-Fi Thriller
The Christmas Planet and Other Stories

Yesterday's Thief: An Eric Beckman Paranormal Sci-Fi Thriller
Sanity's Thief: An Eric Beckman Paranormal Thriller
Democracy's Thief: An Eric Beckman Paranormal Thriller
A Mind Reader's Christmas: An Eric Beckman Mystery
The Day Before Yesterday's Thief: A Prequel to the Eric Beckman Series

The Protected Witness: An Alex Booker Thriller
The Abducted Heiress: An Alex Booker Thriller

About the Author

Al Macy writes because he has stories to tell. In school, he was the class clown and always the first to volunteer for show and tell. His teachers would say, "Al has a lot of imagination." Then they'd roll their eyes.

But he put his storytelling on the back burner until he retired and wrote a blog about his efforts to improve his piano sight-reading. That's when his love of storytelling burbled up to the surface, along with quirky words like "burble."

He had even more fun writing his second book, *Drive, Ride, Repeat*, but was bummed by nonfiction's need to stick to "the truth" (yucko). From then on it was fiction all the way, with a good dose of his science background burbling to the surface.

Macy's top priority is compelling storylines with satisfying plot twists, but he never neglects character development. No, wait … his top priority is quirkiness, then compelling storylines, then character development. No, wait …